Hidden
Lies
Rachel Ryan

PIATKUS

PIATKUS

First published in Great Britain in 2021 by Piatkus
This paperback edition published in 2022 by Piatkus

1 3 5 7 9 10 8 6 4 2

A CIP catalogue record for this book
is available from the British Library.

ISBN 978-0-349-42615-0

Typeset in Bembo by M Rules
Printed and bound in Great Britain by
Clays Ltd, Elcograf S.p.A.

Papers used by Piatkus are from well-managed forests
and other responsible sources.

Piatkus
An imprint of
Little, Brown Book Group
Carmelite House
50 Victoria Embankment
London EC4Y 0DZ

An Hachette UK Company
www.hachette.co.uk

www.littlebrown.co.uk

For Lauren

I

Dublin, Ireland, 2014

On that crisp January afternoon, the park lay silvery and deserted, coated in a thin layer of frost. The grass crunched under Georgina's feet as she followed shrieks of laughter to a cluster of evergreen bushes and trees.

'Boys!' she called towards the bushes. 'Out where I can see you, please!'

Luke and Patrick, her son's friends, tumbled out first. They were giggling, faces flushed so pink Georgina doubted they felt the cold at all.

'Come on, you two, back to the playground.'

They bolted off obediently. But Cody did not emerge.

'Cody?'

Georgina waited. Her breath clouded the air.

'Cody!'

Of course her child would be the defiant one. Georgina sighed.

'Cody, don't make me come in there and get you.'

Still nothing. Luke and Patrick had reached the playground.

Their delighted screams echoed over the otherwise silent fields. A distant dog walker was the only other person in sight.

'*Cody!*'

Just as Georgina was about to push through the branches herself, the leaves shivered, and her son appeared.

Her annoyance melted away in the face of that cheeky half-smile.

'Come on. Your friends are at the playground.' She ruffled his muss of dark hair as they began to walk.

He was sucking on a lollipop he hadn't had earlier.

Georgina frowned. 'Where did you get that?'

Cody took the lollipop out of his mouth. 'The old lady gave it to me.'

'What old lady?'

'The old lady in the bushes.'

He popped it back in his mouth and made to run after his friends. Georgina stopped him.

'You were talking to an old lady in the bushes? Just now?'

Cody nodded, impatient to be off.

'Why would she give you a lollipop, Cody?'

He shrugged. 'She said she was my granny.'

The shiver that travelled down Georgina's spine had nothing to do with the cold. Each hair on the back of her neck stood up as if brushed by a spiderweb.

'Cody,' she said, when she trusted herself to speak, 'that's not right. You know Granny is dead.'

'*I* know that,' Cody said scornfully. '*She* said it. Can I go, Mam, *please*?'

Georgina nodded, too shaken to continue the conversation, and watched him tear off to the playground.

She turned back towards the bushes. They were still. She

looked around the park but could see no one. Even the dog walker had disappeared from sight.

'Patrick, you're on!' Cody was screaming gleefully. 'Catch me if you can, catch me if you can!'

Georgina walked over to the thicket of bushes and trees.

'Hello?'

She took a step closer, then another, and tried peering through the leaves. But all she could see were tree trunks and darkness.

Suddenly self-conscious, she backed away and cut a brisk path to the playground.

'Cody,' she asked, when she managed to pull him away from his friends, 'where did the lollipop really come from?'

'The lady. I told you.' He wriggled out from under her grasp.

'Cody, come on. You shouldn't make up—'

But he was racing back to his friends.

Georgina sat down on a bench.

She said she was my granny.

She wanted to cry. As of last year – 4 July, a date now carved into Georgina's heart – Cody didn't have a grand-mother. Bren's parents had passed away before Cody was born, but Georgina's mother had been a warm, wonderful presence in her grandson's first seven years of life. Now she wouldn't see his eighth birthday.

Georgina wiped away a tear. She didn't know what would compel Cody to say such a thing, but it was upsetting, it was wrong.

'Mam!' Cody was hanging upside down off the climbing frame. 'Look at me, look at *meee*!'

'I see you, sweetie!' Georgina forced a cheerful tone. She

wished now that she hadn't agreed to this play date, but it was too late. Luke and Patrick's respective parents weren't picking them up until seven. Georgina felt tired at the thought.

As they left the park, she looked back over her shoulder, across the icy fields to that lonely patch of trees – and again felt that soft spiderweb brush against the hairs on the back of her neck.

2

'Jesus, that must've been upsetting to hear,' was Bren's reaction when Georgina recounted the story that evening.

'Yeah,' she said. 'It was.'

They were standing in the amber-lit kitchen of their small, slightly shabby, but beloved house. Cosy, Georgina called it. Cramped, Bren said, but affectionately. Their house was in an area of Dublin that was also slightly shabby, but colourful and central and bustling too. 'An area on the up and up!' was how estate agents described it. 'Affordable and close to work' was how Bren and Georgina described it.

Cody was watching TV in the front room, his friends finally gone home.

'I asked Luke and Patrick if they saw anyone in the bushes,' Georgina continued. 'They said no.'

'Well, obviously.' Bren's tone was amused, but warm enough that the words didn't sting. 'What, you thought she might've been real? The ghostly woman in the bushes?'

'No, of course not,' said Georgina. 'I just felt freaked out, I guess. The park was deserted, it was all creepy ... And the thing I couldn't understand was – where did Cody get the lollipop?'

Bren was grinning now. 'Come on, Georgie. You can't think of anywhere Cody might have stolen a lollipop?'

She could, of course: a jar of lollipops stood on Cody's teacher's desk, to be handed out each Friday to the team of seven-year-olds with the most stars for good behaviour that week. Due almost entirely to the fact of Cody and Patrick's membership, Team Orange never won.

'If he'd pocketed it in school, he obviously wouldn't tell you,' Bren pointed out.

'I didn't think of that.' Georgina wondered why this obvious explanation hadn't occurred to her. Had it been the factual manner in which Cody had reported the incident? Or the eerie setting, the quiet park?

'I just felt unsettled,' she concluded. 'After he mentioned my mam.'

'Of course you did.' Bren put an arm around her. 'Anyone would be rattled after hearing that.'

She leant against him. Their embrace was reflected in the kitchen window: Bren six foot two and lanky, with loose brown curls and glasses, and Georgina shorter, slender, with cropped blonde hair and soft features. Bren teased her gently about that haircut, said she could never look edgy no matter how hard she tried; her face was too warm, too approachable.

'It's probably just a game he finds comforting,' Bren continued. 'Just his way of feeling close to Rose.'

A tired, heavy sadness washed over Georgina. 'Yeah, maybe.'

'Children have odd ways of dealing with grief. He didn't

know it would upset you.' Bren kissed her forehead, then moved away to put the kettle on. 'D'you want a cup of tea?'

She nodded.

'Chamomile?'

When she nodded again, he took down her favourite chipped mug. In that instant she felt so comfortable here in their little house with the crammed bookshelves, the potted plants, the crooked lamp in the corner . . .

And the sofa, where Bren had slept when things got really bad between them last year.

'Fancy going to the cinema this weekend?' Bren's voice was a welcome diversion to her train of thought. 'The Light House is showing *Breakfast at Tiffany's*.'

That movie was one of Georgina's favourites; she knew it would never be Bren's choice.

'I can't,' she said with real regret, sitting down at the table. 'I have so much studying to catch up on.'

'You don't have to keep your nose to the grindstone all the time. A couple of hours off would do you good.'

'No, I really can't.'

'No worries.' Bren placed the mug of chamomile tea in front of her. He had been unfailingly supportive, both financially and emotionally, of Georgina's decision to go back to college. However, since her mother's death, he'd expressed concern on several occasions that she had too much on her plate. Georgina didn't disagree, but she didn't know what he expected her to do about it. She was doing the best she could.

'Oh, and I have to find time to visit my dad this weekend,' she remembered. Georgina's father had not been doing well since her mother's death.

'I'll come with you. And we can bring Cody.'

'That'd be nice. Seeing Cody always cheers him up.'

She sipped her tea.

'You know,' said Bren, 'studies suggest that having children doesn't actually make you happier. But people with grand-children are apparently happier than people without.'

'No wonder. You get all the good parts, then you get to hand them back at the end of the day.'

'Exactly.' He grinned. 'One day, we'll be old and grey and Cody will have his own kid and it'll all have been worth it.'

They sat quietly for a while.

Georgina and Bren had met in their early twenties. She had been immediately impressed by him. He had a master's in psychology and a job at a well-known tech company, helping them make their websites more user-friendly. 'I want to work as a psychologist eventually,' he'd told her at the time. 'This is just for a couple of years.' Bren was still in tech.

Georgina, contrastingly, had dropped out of university in her second year (a period of her life she preferred not to think about, even now) and had worked as a retail assistant in a bookshop ever since. When she and Bren met, she had been considering going back to college. But those plans were interrupted by Cody's arrival.

Neither of them had intended to have a child quite so early, in their lives or the relationship. But they adored each other, and Cody, while unexpected, was very welcome. However, it meant Georgina was turning thirty by the time Cody started school and she could return to her own education.

Now she was one year away from being a fully quali-fied teacher.

Studying full-time. Working part-time. And raising her son.

8

'What are you thinking about?'

She zoned back in to the kitchen.

'My mam,' she said. And it was the truth. When she thought about her day-to-day life, she was thinking about how her mother wasn't there to be a part of it. When she thought about college, she was thinking that her mother wouldn't be there to see her graduate. Georgina hadn't stopped thinking about her in the six months since she'd died.

Bren reached out a hand to touch hers.

'I haven't gotten used to the thought of Dad in that big house on his own.' Georgina felt tears fill her eyes. 'God, here I go again with the waterworks. If Mam could see me, she'd tell me to stop my snivelling and get on with it.' How she missed her mother's ability to be warm and no-nonsense at the same time.

'Well, we're going to visit him this weekend, aren't we?'

'Maybe we should bring him over some dinner.' That was what her mother would have done. Focused on something practical. 'I know he's not eating properly.'

'I'll cook something,' Bren offered. He was far more capable in the kitchen than Georgina.

'Thanks.' She smiled at him. He was so good to her, in so many ways. At moments like these, she felt small and petty for being so slow to forgive him that one line he had crossed. After all, he'd only put a *toe* over it, hadn't he?

They were here now, she reminded herself. They were trying.

But after teacups had been tidied away, teeth brushed and Cody tucked into bed, Georgina couldn't bring herself to do the thing she'd been considering all evening: to take Bren by the hand and lead him into the bedroom, to undress and kiss and let go.

It wasn't that she didn't want to. But she wanted to the same way she wanted to go to the gym: she knew she would feel better afterwards, but it was so hard to *start*, so much easier to stare at Netflix and eat Kettle crisps.

She knew Bren wanted to as well – knew this affected him, knew he felt rejected – and that made her feel simultaneously guilty and resentful. They wouldn't be in this situation if not for Bren's toe-over-the-line incident. They'd been doing all right on the sex front before. Maybe not fireworks – they'd been together too long for that – but they'd shared a gentle, familiar intimacy. Now when Georgina reached for those feelings, they just weren't there.

The books and articles she'd been furtively reading on reigniting your love life all emphasised the importance of communication. Georgina didn't feel like communicating with her husband right now. Instead, she spent her evening alternating between studying and scrolling through social media sites.

She and Bren went to bed at the same time, as they did most nights. Georgina was getting changed into her comfortable old nightdress, and Bren was in the bathroom brushing his teeth, when the house phone rang.

The momentary pang of worry she felt if the phone rang late at night – was it her father? was something wrong? – had become a familiar one to Georgina since her mother's passing. She glanced at the screen. Caller ID hidden.

'Hello?'

Silence on the line.

'Dad? Is that you?'

It was a deliberate silence, somehow. It gave Georgina the odd but definite sense that someone was listening on the other end.

She felt a sudden, absolute certainty that it was not her father.

'Who is this?'

Bren dropped something in the bathroom with a loud clatter, and Georgina jolted. She hung up the phone. You're being silly, she told herself as she got under the covers. But she couldn't help wishing Bren would come back into the room.

He did, moments later. Switching off the lights, he settled in the bed beside her, warm and solid and smelling of soap. 'Who was on the phone?'

'Prank call, I think. There was someone on the line, but they didn't say anything.'

'Kids still do prank calls nowadays? How very nineties.'

He draped an arm around her waist. All the sex they weren't having couldn't change this: the familiar shape their bodies made, tucked together like spoons for almost a decade now. Despite the things that had faltered between them in the past year, physical affection remained, and this gave Georgina hope that they could get back to where they'd once been.

'Spooked you, didn't it?' Bren could always read her mood.

'I just hate calls at night. I always think the worst.' She relaxed against him. 'And I was surprised when the house phone rang.' Neither she nor Bren ever used it, relying on their smartphones for everything.

'We should get rid of it.' Bren yawned. 'The thing's prehistoric.'

He wasn't wrong. Their house phone was an ancient block of a thing that did not record the date or time of calls, only the number.

Within minutes Bren was snoring, a low, comforting

rumble. Georgina lay awake a while longer, listening to the winter wind outside. It gusted and howled, and sent tree branches scratching against windows, like fingers searching for a way in.

3

On her way to collect Cody from school the next day, Georgina stopped off at the park.

The playground was deserted again. The football fields glittered white. One dedicated lone jogger circled the park's perimeter. Otherwise, there was no one in sight.

As she approached the thicket of bushes where Cody claimed to have seen the old lady, Georgina felt half embarrassed. She wasn't sure what had compelled her to come back here. She knew she was being ridiculous.

But she couldn't quite shake that feeling that had shivered down her spine.

Embarrassment intensifying, Georgina steeled herself and – glad that there was nobody around to see – ducked down like a child and pushed under the icy branches.

When she straightened up, she found herself in a shadowy clearing. It was scattered with litter: discarded beer cans, cigarette ends, a single shoe ... A circle of blackened earth marked where somebody had lit a fire.

But it was quiet now. Whoever came here at night was elsewhere.

Georgina was alone.

She turned on the spot, looking all around. The bushes were dense, the tree trunks thick. It was possible an adult could have stood concealed behind one of those trees, out of sight of Luke and Patrick, stepping out only when Cody was alone ...

A breeze sent the leaves rustling, and Georgina shivered.

She said she was my granny.

Just as she shook herself, determined not to get spooked, the branches to her right trembled.

She turned her head sharply. Could that have been the wind?

No, because the wind was in the leaves, softly whispering. Whatever was moving in the bushes was deliberate, solid.

A twig cracked.

Georgina took a step back. From the looks of this place, she didn't want to meet any of the people who frequented it.

But something was coming. The sounds were getting closer now, crashing towards her—

Then, sending all the branches shuddering, a shape tumbled out onto the ground.

A huge woolly white dog with a lolling pink tongue and wagging tail.

'Oh my God.' Georgina crouched down to rub his head. 'You scared me, boy.'

The dog licked her hand happily before charging off into the undergrowth.

She straightened up. Get it together, she told herself.

Nobody had been lurking behind any trees. The fictional grandmother was just Cody's way of dealing with grief, as Bren had said. The phone call last night had been a prank or a wrong number.

She was getting anxious over nothing.

As she turned to leave, Georgina noticed a glimmer of gold on the rubbish-strewn ground. Something stamped into the dirt.

Hesitantly, she reached down and pinched it between her thumb and forefinger. As delicately as she could, she tugged it free.

But it was only a golden sweet wrapper, with the words CAFFREY'S CONFECTIONERY stamped across it. She let it drift back to the ground.

For God's sake, said the part of her brain that sometimes spoke in Bren's firm, rational voice. *You're letting a child's imagination get under your skin.*

Picturing the look that would be on his face as he said it, she decided not to mention to Bren that she'd come here.

Feeling idiotic, and suddenly very aware of how cold it was, Georgina wrapped her scarf tighter around her neck and set off to collect her son from school.

4

Later that afternoon, when Cody was settled in front of the TV, Georgina sat at the kitchen table and opened her laptop to study. But she couldn't concentrate.

Closing her eyes, she envisioned her future as an art teacher. A brightly lit classroom, with paintings on the walls. An end, finally, to shift work. Finding the odd student with real promise, seeing them go on to complete their degree as she hadn't . . . Focusing on that dream always gave her the motivation to get to work. But—

'Mam?' Just as she began to type, Cody burst into the room. 'I'm bored of watching TV.'

Feeling like the Worst Mother in the World, Georgina said, 'How about half an hour more TV? Just one more episode and—'

Ding-dong.

'I'll get it!' Delighted by the distraction, Cody went thumping into the hall. Resigned, Georgina followed him.

She found him on the doorstep talking to Vera, their next-door neighbour.

'Hiya, Georgina!' Vera was a small, warm woman in her seventies. With her round face and round glasses, she always put Georgina vaguely in mind of an owl. She was wearing a puffy purple coat, and her permed hair was dyed a dull fair colour that Georgina guiltily thought of as old-lady blonde. It was her mother, Rose, who had put that phrase in her head: *Don't ever let them put that old-lady blonde in my hair! It's worse than grey.* Georgina had found her mother's commitment to glamour an endearing vanity. Rose wouldn't have been caught dead in a coat like the one Vera was wearing.

The phrase *caught dead* jarred in Georgina's mind.

'I baked too much, as usual,' Vera was saying. 'Banana bread, straight from the oven.'

'Well come on in!' said Cody importantly. Georgina had to smile. Vera's habit of showing up with baked goods made her very popular with Cody.

Until recently, Vera had shared her home with her daughter, Lorraine, Lorraine's partner Dave and their two-year-old son, Sean. But Lorraine, Dave and Sean had emigrated and moved to Australia late last year.

Georgina had liked Lorraine and Dave. Small houses and thin walls created a sense of intimacy and Georgina, who'd overheard their jokes, arguments and laughter, knew they were a happy family. When they left, Vera had maintained a determinedly cheery outlook, but Georgina knew it must be difficult for her. That noisy house suddenly empty. All the family she had on the other side of the world.

In the kitchen, Cody and Vera sat down at the table while Georgina put the kettle on.

'How are Lorraine and Dave getting on?' she asked Vera as she made the tea.

'Oh, they're getting on great,' Vera said, unwrapping the bread. 'There's far more opportunity for young people over there, you know.'

The instant the banana bread was uncovered, Cody grabbed a slice and shoved it into his mouth.

'Cody,' Georgina chided.

Vera only chuckled. 'I was on Skype to them this morning,' she went on. 'Lorraine was terrified because Sean found a huge spider in the house, but Sean wasn't scared at all. "I saw big spidey, Nanny," he kept saying. "Big spidey!"'

'How big was the spider?' Cody demanded through a mouthful of banana bread.

'Huge,' said Vera solemnly. 'Big as your hand.'

'Gross,' said Cody with enthusiasm. 'Was it poisonous?'

'Well, probably not,' Vera admitted. 'But,' she continued, lowering her voice to a dramatic whisper, 'some of the spiders over there are *deadly* poisonous.'

As Vera and Cody discussed Australian wildlife, Georgina zoned out to the *tick-tock* of the kitchen clock.

She thought of her behaviour earlier. Climbing into the bushes like an idiot. Scared half to death by a dog, for God's sake. She thought about getting back to her studies once Vera was gone. She thought, as she did constantly, about her mother. She stifled a yawn, sipped her chamomile tea and watched the clock *tick-tock* as Vera chatted.

The shadows. The clock. The stuffed toy.

An involuntary shudder ran through her. That was a most unwelcome memory, one she pushed firmly away. Why would she think of that now? Her spine stiffened, causing her to sit up straighter in her chair, but neither Vera nor Cody, deep in conversation, seemed to notice.

'. . . and poisonous snakes that crawl into shoes,' Vera was telling Cody. 'People put on their shoes and feel something wriggling . . . '

Georgina had to smile at the look of delight on Cody's face. Never underestimate the bloodthirstiness of the average seven-year-old. Feeling a little better, she helped herself to a slice of banana bread. It was soft and delicious.

When the tea was finished and the table cleared, Georgina walked Vera to the door. 'Pop over anytime, Vera.'

'You're very good, Georgina. Talk to you soon.'

After Vera had gone indoors, Georgina lingered in her own front garden a moment longer, wanting to breathe in the crisp air and outside world before returning to her laptop.

Across the street, the Brazilian couple from number 24 walked with arms around each other, laughing at some private joke. The woman was heavily pregnant. Her partner held her with a tenderness that tugged at Georgina's chest. They were part of the backdrop to her neighbourhood. Just like the students in number 18, who never mowed their lawn and sometimes threw wild parties. Just like Anthony, their next-door neighbour on the other side: a burly man, sixty-ish, with faded tattoos and a heavily lined face. Unlike Vera, Anthony had always lived alone. He could come across gruff – Bren had never liked him – but Georgina thought there was kindness in the lines around his eyes. She always gave him a warm smile, and sometimes she got one in return.

Georgina loved living here. Loved the red-brick houses and the twisted tree roots that split the concrete. Loved that a five-minute walk to the left reached a bustling main road, busy with pubs and bakeries and flower shops, but that her street was quiet and calm. A slice of an old neighbourhood in the heart of Dublin.

She took it all in, then turned and walked indoors. Back to the grindstone. But first, where was . . .

'Cody?'

Not in the kitchen. Georgina went to check the front room. The TV was off. No sign of him.

Just as she was about to leave the room, she heard a small noise behind the sofa.

She smiled.

'I wonder where Cody could be hiding,' she addressed the room.

In the ensuing silence, she heard that sound again – a secretive scuffle.

'Under the table? No . . .' Georgina walked with deliberately clunky footsteps across the floor. 'Behind the door? No . . . Could he be behind the sofa?'

She leant over the top of the sofa and saw her son crouching there, the house phone pressed to his ear.

'Hi, Mam,' Cody said. Then he added into the phone: 'She found me.'

Georgina felt her smile fade a little.

'Who are you talking to, sweetie?'

Cody giggled.

'Is the phone for me, Cody?' she asked, a little more sternly.

'*No!*' For a child with a tendency to misbehave, Cody became very indignant when wrongfully accused. 'It's for me.'

'Who is it?'

He was grinning like this was an enormous joke, one he

hadn't decided whether or not to let his mother in on yet. Then . . .

'It's the old lady,' he said. 'From the park. The old lady who wants to be my granny.'

The sudden trembling inside Georgina was so strong she was surprised to see that her hand, when she held it out, was quite steady.

'Cody,' she said, her tone leaving no room for disagreement, 'give me the phone.'

He heard the change in her voice and reluctantly handed it over. Georgina hesitated for a fraction of a second, remembering that late-night phone call, that deliberate silence on the line, before holding the handset to her ear.

'Hello?'

Nobody there. Just a dial tone.

She shook her head inwardly at her own overactive imagination. She was sorry now for interrupting Cody's game. 'I think Granny must have hung up, darling,' she said.

Cody grabbed the phone back, and his face fell. 'She *did* hang up.' He looked up at Georgina accusingly. 'Maybe she doesn't like you.'

5

They visited Georgina's father on Saturday, as planned. Georgina's childhood home was considerably bigger than the one she lived in now, located in an area considerably swankier than the one she lived in now.

'Georgie,' her father boomed at the door, folding her into a big hug. 'My great girl.'

Jimmy McGrath was a huge man – massively tall and broad, and, in his old age, fat with it, due to his fondness for red wine and rich food. He had towered over his late wife, a tiny woman who had nevertheless been the tougher of the two.

'How're you doing, Dad?'

'Ah, grand, grand,' Jimmy said loudly. 'Can't complain. What's that you have there, Bren?'

Bren was carrying the dinner in Tupperware containers. 'Chicken Alfredo made with cauliflower sauce.'

Jimmy eyed it suspiciously. He approved of Bren, but not what he called his 'fancy cooking'. 'Cauliflower sauce?' he muttered to Georgina. 'I never heard the likes.' Then, leaning down from his great height towards Cody, he asked: 'And how's my favourite grandson?'

'I'm your only grandson,' Cody answered as he always answered, and Jimmy laughed as he always laughed, a great booming ha-ha-ha, before slipping Cody a twenty-euro note.

'Oh for God's sake, Dad,' said Georgina, amused and exasperated in equal measure. 'You gave him twenty quid last weekend too. He's seven; he doesn't need all that money.'

'I do *so* need it,' said Cody, and with the note clutched happily in one hand, he raced inside and began jumping up and down on the sofa. Jimmy smiled indulgently, unfazed by the threat to his expensive furniture.

'There you are. He does need it. What are you going to buy, Cody?'

'I'm going to buy the Mega-Power Purple Slinger Machine Gun with penguin and monkey bullets!'

'Well, there you have it, Georgie. He's going to buy the Mega-Purple ... what was it?'

'Slinger Machine Gun,' Bren interjected in passing. 'Some awful toy all the kids are mad for. Costs nearly two hundred quid.'

'Well then,' said Jimmy loudly, '*I'll* buy it for him.'

'Shh,' Georgina hushed him. Luckily Cody, still jumping on the sofa, hadn't heard. 'Dad, he got a ton of toys for Christmas. Why don't you wait till his birthday?'

'But I don't mind buying it.'

'That's really good of you, but there's just no need. And he doesn't need money every time we pop around either.'

'Georgina,' said her father huffily, 'I've *always* given Cody money when he visits.'

23

'And I appreciate it. But when Mam was still here, we didn't visit quite so—'

Georgina broke off. At the mention of his late wife, Jimmy's jolly mask slipped, and what was hidden behind it shocked her. He looked so grey, so grief-stricken, so old.

'Dad.' She felt suddenly sick. What was she arguing for? If spoiling his grandchild bought her father some happiness, brought some light to that exhausted face, surely it was money well spent.

'Buy him the stupid toy, Dad.' Let him spoil Cody rotten. 'I'm sorry I made a fuss.'

Georgina thought suddenly of Cody's pretend phone call and prayed he wouldn't mention that awful game in front of his grandfather. She didn't think Jimmy could handle hearing Rose's memory being used in such a flippant and disturbing manner.

'Dad? Are you listening to me?' She touched his arm. 'Get him the Mega-Power Purple Slinger Machine Gun if you want.'

Jimmy looked at her, and the hint of a smile creased his eyes. Georgina could have cried with relief.

'The Purple Monkey what? Am I expected to remember the bloody name?'

Georgina started to giggle – and then they were both laughing, the kind of laughter that gathers momentum, has a life of its own. They clutched each other, hysterical, until Cody came over to stare with some concern. 'What are you laughing at?'

Georgina wiped tears from her eyes. 'Purple ... monkey ... ' she managed, and then they were off again.

Cody shook his head soberly. 'Grown-ups are weird.'

*

The dinner was delicious. Jimmy, despite his reservations regarding cauliflower sauce, cleared his plate and asked for more.

As they were loading the dishwasher afterwards, Georgina said to her father, 'I noticed a lot of cardboard boxes upstairs.' She didn't mention that she had looked inside the boxes and recognised her mother's clothes.

'Oh, those,' Jimmy replied as he scraped leftovers into the bin. 'Old stuff that needs to be sorted. Most of it'll go to charity, I suppose.' He did not look at her as he spoke.

'I can help, Dad,' Georgina offered. 'I'll come round and go through some of the stuff for you.'

'Would you, love?' He looked at her gratefully then. 'That'd be great.'

Before they left, Georgina slipped out to the back garden. Her mother had always left food and water out for wild animals. Since her death, Jimmy had pledged to keep her birdfeeders filled. But while his intentions were good, his efforts were haphazard, and Georgina knew that more often than not he simply forgot.

Today she found the feeders empty and the water iced over. Quietly, without pointing it out to her father, she refilled them both.

On the way home, Bren drove. Georgina stared out the window and thought about her father in that big house by himself. His wife was gone. His brother Billy, his only sibling, had been in a home with early-onset Alzheimer's for several years now. She thought of Jimmy with just the TV for company. She thought of her mother's birds going hungry.

She would visit her father more often. Help him with

the boxes of clothes. Fill the birdfeeders herself. What else could she do?

She had not realised that Bren had overheard her conversation with her dad, but later that evening, he brought it up.

'It won't be an easy job, Georgina, helping your dad sort through Rose's things.'

Cody was upstairs. They were in the kitchen. Bren was chopping carrots, meal-prepping for the week ahead.

'I know.' Tired, Georgina leant against the counter. 'But you know he won't do it himself. Those boxes will just sit there forever.'

'D'you ever notice how you seem to find the time to look after everyone except yourself?'

Bren's point was valid. Helping Jimmy clear out Rose's things would be taxing in more ways than one. But this topic of conversation was beginning to wear on her. It felt like nagging.

Or maybe her irritation was simply due to the fact that there was something spiky between them these past months. Things hadn't been the same, not since ...

Georgina tried to rein in her train of thought, but it was too late. Emma's face popped into her mind in perfect detail. Glossy dark hair. Green eyes. Sharp cheekbones. She hated that she could picture Emma so clearly. She hated that it still hit her as hard, as suddenly, as this.

' ... and milk and bread for tomorrow,' Bren was saying.

'What?' Georgina zoned back in.

'We're out of milk and bread.'

Bread they could live without, but milk was essential. Cody refused to eat anything but cereal in the mornings.

'I'll pop up to the shops.' She felt a sudden, visceral need to get away from her husband.

'I can go. It's—'

'No, really. I'd like the walk.' She avoided looking directly at him. She was ashamed of how overwhelming this sudden anger was.

Petty. Small.

Those were the words with which Georgina berated herself as she walked to the shops, bundled up in her warmest coat and scarf. It was a clear night. Ice glittered on car windscreens. A crescent moon hung delicate and white in the black sky.

Let it go.

Walking back, with the milk in her bag, she reflected on this. She *wanted* to let it go, to release that sharp shard of anger she was still holding onto. But how? How did people learn the art of letting go?

Lost in thought, she turned her key in the lock and stepped into her home.

'Georgie.' Bren met her in the hall, speaking in a whisper. 'Come here.'

'What's up?' Instinctively responding in hushed tones, she followed him to the kitchen.

Bren took a deep breath. 'I don't want you to get upset.'

This sent an alert running through her.

'What is it?'

'Cody is pretending to be on the phone to his grand-mother again.'

Georgina froze.

'I know,' said Bren. 'I know it's—'

'Where is he?'

'The front room.'

She dropped her bag on the table and made for the hall.

'Georgina.' Bren spoke quietly, but with a timbre that caused her to pause. 'Where are you going?'

'I just want to check on him.'

Bren's brow furrowed. 'All right,' he said. 'But let's be careful not to disturb him, okay?'

Together they tiptoed down the hall and peered through the half-open door into the front room. Cody was on the sofa, with his back to them. Phone to his ear, he chatted away, oblivious to their gaze.

There was something about his giggles and long pauses in conversation that made it seem very, very real.

Bren put a finger to his lips and beckoned Georgina. They tiptoed back to the kitchen. Once out of Cody's earshot, he said, 'It makes me feel uncomfortable too. But he used to talk to Rose on the phone all the time, and he must miss that.'

Georgina, only half listening, was looking around for the other house phone. In that moment, she didn't care how silly she was being. Nothing would give her greater peace than to listen in on Cody chatting away to a dead line.

'Where's the other house phone?'

'I don't know.' Bren shrugged. 'Under a pile of laundry somewhere, out of battery.'

Okay. She was just going to say it.

'How do we know for sure he's not really on the phone to someone?'

Concern softened Bren's features.

'Georgie, come here. Sit down.' He steered her to the sofa in the kitchen corner. 'Take a few deep breaths.'

She complied.

'Right.' His voice was declarative. 'For one thing, there's

the simple fact that it's impossible for Cody to be on the phone to his grandmother . . .'

Georgina opened her mouth to protest – she had never suggested anything *supernatural* was going on and felt insulted by the insinuation – but Bren was still talking.

'. . . and anyway,' he said with finality, 'the phone didn't *ring*, Georgina. I would have heard it.'

Georgina considered this. She looked at Bren's earnest face. His hair, damp from the shower, looked almost black. His eyes looked bluer when his hair was darkened like that, blue and serious. He reached for her. She hesitated a moment longer, then let him pull her close. Let herself be soothed.

'I know this is difficult,' he said. 'But seven-year-olds play imaginary games. We have to let Cody grieve in his own way.'

Georgina nodded, though she had to suppress the urge to march into the front room and grab the phone from Cody's hand.

6

No matter how quickly she rushed from the bookshop at the end of her shift, the dash to pick Cody up from school was tight, and Georgina didn't always make it on time. Cody hated being the last child left.

You're working, studying and mothering, she told herself, as she struggled to find parking. Being a few minutes late once in a while doesn't make you a failure.

But it wasn't enough to dissipate the guilt, and she was relieved to find a spot on the next street over, which allowed her to arrive at the gates out of breath and ruffled, but with two minutes to spare.

'Hiya, Georgina!'

'Hi, Kelly-Anne.'

Kelly-Anne, Patrick's mother, was never ruffled. Her jet-black hair hung silky-straight to her waist (Georgina presumed some of that glossy mane must be fake, but it was hard to tell). Her make-up looked like it had been done by professionals. She was always immaculately turned out – the tan, the nails, the eyeshadow/earring/handbag colour coordination. The attention to detail made Georgina feel dizzy. She could never understand where Kelly-Anne found the time.

'Good Christmas, Georgina? Did you get away at all?'

Georgina's first Christmas without her mother had been a low-key, difficult affair. 'No, we stayed in Dublin.'

'Ah, did you? Lovely time, though?' Kelly-Anne asked a lot of questions but rarely paused to listen to the answers. 'Myself and Mark spent a week in Dubai. Not very Christmassy, ha-ha-ha, but it was gorgeous. Got a great colour.'

She pulled up her sleeve to show Georgina her deeply tanned arm.

'Did Cody enjoy his holidays? Patrick got one of those bloody Mega-Power Purple Slinger things and spent all Christmas Day firing little plastic animals at everyone.'

Georgina had to laugh.

The school door opened, and children came pouring out, Cody and Patrick pushing to the front.

'Mam!' Cody burst out. 'Can I go to Patrick's house today, *please*?'

'Well I don't know, sweetie.' Georgina had been looking forward to spending the afternoon with her son. But before she could gently suggest that Patrick come over at the weekend instead, Kelly-Anne swooped in.

'Oh, it's no bother, Georgina. He's welcome.'

'Yes!' The two boys jumped up and down with happiness, then raced off, Kelly-Anne drifting after them.

'I can drop him home if picking him up is a hassle,' she called. 'Just give me a text and let me know.'

And she was gone, leaving a blast of overly sweet perfume

in her wake and Georgina with nothing to do but say: 'Great. Thanks then,' rather lamely, and a few beats too late.

With Cody at Patrick's, Georgina had all afternoon to study uninterrupted. Notes spread across the table, eating peanut butter off a spoon, she knew she should be appreciative of this rare opportunity to relax like a twenty-year-old student.

Still, she missed Cody. And by the time she texted Kelly-Anne to tell her she was on her way, she couldn't wait for her son's noisy chatter to fill up the house again.

When she arrived to collect him, he was hyper and bouncy and high-pitched.

'Did you have fun with Patrick, sweetie?' she asked as they walked home hand-in-hand along the pavement.

'Yes! We went to the park, and we saw lots of dogs, and a pigeon nearly flew into Patrick's head, and . . .'

She smiled at him wryly. 'And I'd say you ate some sweets, did you?'

'Lots! Patrick's mam bought us ice cream, *and* fizzy green bars that make your tongue go tingly.'

'Hmm,' said Georgina, not wanting to know what ingredients went into those.

'And guess who I saw in the park?'

'Who?'

'New Granny!'

Georgina's stomach jolted. She forced herself to keep walking, keep smiling. She remembered Bren's words: *We have to let Cody grieve in his own way.*

'Did you?' was all she could think to say.

'Yes. She gave me a chocolate bar.'

Feeling ridiculously clichéd, Georgina said, 'Cody, if a real stranger ever offers you sweets, you say "No thank you" – you know that, right?'

'Why? She wants to be my granny and I said okay because I don't have any grannies now.' Cody was hopping over the cracks in the pavement, and his hand nearly slid out of hers. Georgina held on tighter.

'You told her she could be your granny?'

'Well, she *is* an old lady,' said Cody reasonably. 'So I said she could be New Granny.'

He was concentrating hard on avoiding the cracks. She had to compose herself before saying, 'This is a game, Cody, right?'

'No,' said Cody casually, without looking at her. 'It's real.'

'Where's the chocolate bar, then?'

'I ate it.' Cody was still focused on his steps. Georgina tugged at his hand.

'Cody. Then where's the wrapper?'

'I don't know. Let *go*, Mam. You're pulling me.'

She released him. 'Sorry, sweetie.'

He went back to jumping over the cracks, and she walked alongside him in silence for a bit.

'Sweetie, you weren't really on the phone the other night, were you?'

'I was! I was talking to New Granny.'

'Cody, you can tell me the truth. I won't be annoyed. Pretend games don't count as lying.'

'It's *not* pretend!'

Georgina ruffled his hair gently, unsure how to proceed. 'Okay, so it was real,' she said, treading carefully, 'but the phone didn't really *ring*, did it?'

'It did ring,' Cody said serenely. 'You were at the shops and Dad was in the shower.'

Georgina did stop walking now. Had Bren had a shower the previous evening? She couldn't remember. And even if he had, that didn't prove anything. It was probably just a detail Cody was using to embellish his story.

'Mam?'

Cody was looking up at her with big eyes, and Georgina felt suddenly ashamed. Bren's voice echoed in her head once more: *He used to talk to Rose on the phone all the time, and he must miss that.*

She took her son's hand again. 'Tell me about your afternoon with Patrick. What else did you two get up to?'

The next day, at the school gates, Kelly-Anne appeared in a pink faux-fur coat that was enormous in volume. She looked like a fuzzy cloud over legs.

'Nice coat,' said Georgina, only because it was impossible not to comment on it.

'Oh thanks! Mark nearly killed me when he saw the price tag, but I just couldn't resist!' Kelly-Anne launched into a detailed story about a spending spree she had gone on in New York. Georgina nodded along, waiting for Kelly-Anne to pause for breath.

'I wanted to ask you something,' she said when an opening occurred. 'It's kind of a weird question, actually.'

That caught Kelly-Anne's attention. She waited, peering at Georgina from beneath false eyelashes.

'You didn't see an old woman talking to Cody in the park yesterday, did you?'

'What?' Kelly-Anne blinked at her.

'I know it sounds odd, but ... you didn't notice a grey-haired woman hanging around at all?'

'In the park? No. Why?' Kelly-Anne's lipsticked mouth was an O of curiosity. 'What old woman?'

'It's nothing. Forget it.' Georgina tried to wave a hand airily, but she could feel herself going red. 'I think Cody's going through a phase of making up stories.'

Kelly-Anne was clearly about to ask something further, but Georgina was saved when Cody rushed over. 'Hi, Mam!'

'We'd better be off.' She seized her son's hand gratefully. 'Thanks again for the play date yesterday, Kelly-Anne.'

As they walked away, Georgina felt unsatisfied by the conversation. She had been somewhat hopeful Kelly-Anne would say: 'What? We didn't go to the park at all yesterday!' Then she would have known for certain that Cody was making all of this up.

Which he was. Of course he was. But she'd feel comforted by some definitive proof, all the same.

7

Infidelity, Georgina and Bren had promised each other long ago, was unforgivable. 'Any cheating and it's over' had seemed straightforward in the haze of twenty-something love by the firelight of their first home in Phibsboro.

But when Bren had confessed to putting a toe over that line, years had passed, and much had changed.

On an ordinary Wednesday evening last spring, he'd turned to her out of the blue and blurted out, 'I can't not tell you.' His mood had been low since the weekend, but Georgina had put it down to an extended hangover.

Bren had been on a hiking trip with a group of friends from university. They'd walked part of the Wicklow Way, and spent Saturday night in a hotel. Georgina had encouraged him to go. That was what they did for each other: took turns taking care of Cody so they could each have experiences outside parenthood. 'You don't go hiking enough any more. You used to love it.' She had kissed him goodbye at the door and told him to have a great time. She had not let herself become preoccupied with the fact that Emma would be there.

Emma. Bren's long-ago girlfriend from his university days. Dark-haired, green-eyed, petite, pretty Emma, for whom Georgina had suspected Bren still felt a faint attraction. However, it hadn't particularly bothered her. After all, she still thought dreamily of her first boyfriend from time to time. Still felt a sweet nostalgia for that long hot summer when she was seventeen, which felt like a movie now, scenes from someone else's life. It had no bearing on her relationship with Bren: real, solid, tangible.

She had thought they were above such petty things as jealousy. Had thought herself wonderfully mature and sensible.

'It just happened.' Bren's face, across the kitchen table, was all crumpled and sorry. 'It was a stupid, drunken mistake. We got to the hotel, we went to the pub ... Christ, we were pissed. Emma and me were the last ones awake ...'

Georgina felt like her heart had turned to ice.

'You slept together?'

'No – no! It was just drunken kissing, that's all. For maybe half an hour, then I sobered up and realised what I was doing and went to bed.'

She would wonder later if he had deliberately told the story that way so that her anger would be mitigated by relief. If so, it had worked – to an extent.

But Georgina knew the kind of kissing that happened between old lovers at 2 a.m. The hungry, urgent, pressed-up-against-a-wall kind. The kind that happened not in marital beds but in dimly lit bars, in hotel rooms. The relentless desire that could only be found in stolen moments.

She herself had given up that kind of secret, stolen kissing;

37

considered it a fair trade for the security and happiness she had found with Bren.

How it burned to think he'd been kissing someone else like that. While she was at home looking after their child, doing the laundry, putting away his socks. Sending him a message that said:

Send me some photos of the views! Hope you're having a great time xxx

Christ, reading that afterwards was humiliating. Had Bren glanced at his phone, felt guilty, then returned to groping his ex-girlfriend?

'Promise me nothing else happened.'

'That's all, Georgina, and even that's killing me. I feel sick to my stomach whenever I think about it. I'd do anything to take it back.'

Twenty-something Georgina might have called her a doormat, but thirty-something Georgina knew that the days they'd promised each other *any cheating and it's over* were long ago in more ways than one. What was she supposed to do – throw away her marriage over a drunken kiss, over half an hour?

In the following days, her anger came in waves. She tried not to torture herself too much with thoughts of precisely where hands might have been during that half an hour. She tried to remind herself this was a small blip in the life-long story of a marriage. And her efforts to keep her feelings in perspective were working, more or less – until the phone call she received that Friday.

It was her mother. She said 'hospital'. She said 'tests'. And she said that one word beginning with C that nobody ever wants to hear.

Georgina's world fell apart.

'Why didn't you tell me you were going for tests, Mam?'

'Oh, you know. I didn't want to worry you if it turned out to be nothing.' Rose had sounded light-hearted, breezy; that was how she faced tragedy. 'But I'm afraid it is something after all.'

Georgina's anger at Bren's slip-up mixed with her fear and grief until she didn't know where one emotion ended and another began. How could he have driven this wedge between them at the very moment she needed him most? How could he?

Of course, when Bren decided to put his tongue in Emma's mouth, he'd had no idea those test results were hanging over them. No idea that later that week his wife would learn her mother had been diagnosed with cancer. Georgina would never forget his stricken expression when he heard. She knew it was the timing that made him look like a bigger bastard than he was – and yet. If he just *hadn't*. That was the train of thought she tortured herself with. If he just hadn't done it in the first place! If he'd just acted like the married man he was!

The following months were the worst of Georgina's life. Rose, who had decided against chemo, grew sicker with frightening speed. Within weeks, she was shrunken, barely able to move for the pain. Georgina, who had anticipated a long-drawn-out battle, had been shell-shocked by the sheer *pace* of her illness. It wasn't a battle so much as an annihilation.

During that traumatic time, she put aside the issue of Bren and Emma's drunken kiss. It felt small and embarrassing. It was the last thing she wanted to bring up when her mother had this huge, terrifying monster to face.

And within eleven weeks of her diagnosis, Rose was gone.

In the time since, Georgina had often regretted not asking for her mother's opinion. She wished she knew what Rose would have said. Would she have called Bren an arsehole and advised Georgina to be harder on him? Or would she have told her daughter that marriage was long and monogamy difficult and she should make room for these kinds of missteps? Both seemed plausible responses for Rose, who had never been one to hold back from saying what she really felt.

Now six months had passed, and Bren was trying, tentatively, to breach the distance that had grown between them.

They had an evening in planned for Saturday. Just the two of them. Cody was sleeping over at his grandfather's, and Bren suggested that he and Georgina do something nice. 'We'll have the house to ourselves. I'll make dinner.'

Georgina was content with Cody staying at her father's. Jimmy had bought his grandson the Mega-Power Purple Slinger Machine Gun, and if Cody was going to spend all day shooting tiny plastic penguins and monkeys around, she was happy for him to do so in someone else's home.

She was less enthused about her and Bren's plans for the evening. *Date night*. The very thought made Georgina want to groan and change into her most comfortable, least sexy clothes.

But she tried to appreciate the effort Bren was making. He was cooking. He'd bought candles.

She should meet him halfway.

Before Cody went to his grandfather's, Bren had a gentle

talk with him. 'Remember, buddy, while you're with Grandad, I need you not to mention your pretend granny game, okay?'

'It's not a game!' Cody replied indignantly. 'She's real!'

'Okay, buddy. She's real. But don't mention her to Grandad. It might make him upset.'

Cody promised. And Georgina, listening at the door, felt that same cold shiver creep through her. It disturbed her to hear how vehemently Cody insisted his 'new granny' was real.

But once he was gone, she tried to put thoughts of Cody's creepy game out of her head. As she showered and dressed, she gave herself a talking-to. Bren was downstairs cooking and lighting candles; the least she could do was *try*, dammit.

She dug out a dress she hadn't worn in two years and pulled it on over the matching black underwear she'd bought the day before. *Underwear that makes you feel sexy* had been recommended in many of the articles she'd read.

Her cropped hair was growing out a little, overdue for a trim, but she could ruffle it with her fingertips into a messy style she liked. As she applied red lipstick and slipped on high heels, she felt absurdly self-conscious, like she was playing dress-up. She kicked off the heels, hesitated, then put them back on again.

When Bren saw her, he let out a low whistle. 'Wow.'

Georgina was equally impressed. 'Bren, this is amazing!'

Every surface was covered in candles, the whole room lit by flickering light.

'You like it?' He looked anxious, and Georgina, feeling a rush of tenderness, wanted to reassure him.

'It's beautiful.' She sat down at the candlelit table. Visibly pleased, he poured her a glass of wine.

The food was good, the wine light and crisp. Conversation flowed, prickly topics were avoided, and by the end of the meal they were laughing easily together.

But when they moved to the sofa and began kissing, Georgina couldn't lose herself in the moment. She tried, but it wasn't working for her. As they kissed, she was completely in her own head, aware of what was happening and unconvinced by it.

Even if you're not a hundred per cent in the mood, try and go with it! one article had recommended. *You'll get there!*

Bren unzipped her dress and sat behind her, kissing her neck the way she liked, but she still couldn't *feel* it. Just as she was thinking she wouldn't be able to *get there*, just as she was wondering whether she and Bren were permanently broken, his lips began to trace her spine, brushing delicately down her back, sending delicious shivers across her skin . . .

And suddenly her body was awake and alive and excited and didn't care about her mind at all.

When he moved her gently onto her back, it felt just like it used to. When they kissed, hard, it was like they were themselves again, if only for a moment. Bren smiled at her, then began kissing his way down her belly. She relaxed into it, resting her head back in anticipation. Candlelight flickered over the ceiling she wouldn't be able to focus on in a moment, as Bren inched her underwear down towards her knees, and Georgina let her head fall sideways and saw . . .

Somebody standing at the window, looking in.

Georgina screamed. Bren fell back into a half-sitting position as she lunged forward, pulling her underwear back up.

'What's wrong?'

'There's someone in the garden!' She pointed to the

42

window. Bren, who was still wearing jeans, rushed over to press his face against the glass.

'There's nobody out there,' he said. 'It was probably a trick of the light. The candles . . .'

'No. There was someone watching us, I *saw* them.'

'Okay,' he said, moving to the back door, 'I'll go outside and have a look.'

'*No!*' she said, too forcefully. 'Please don't.'

Zipping up her dress, she approached the window cautiously. She could see nothing out there now but darkness.

'I'm not imagining things, Bren. There was somebody there.'

'I'll just go and check,' he said soothingly.

Georgina didn't want to be soothed. She wanted to be taken seriously. She stood back, tense, as Bren opened the door, sending icy air through the warm room.

She turned off the low music that had been playing. In the silence, she could hear Bren moving around in the back garden. The scuffle of his feet. The sound of him opening and closing the side gate.

After a few moments, he sauntered back in and declared, 'There's nobody there.'

She sat down shakily on the sofa. Bren eased in beside her and put an arm around her.

'The side gate was locked,' he said. 'It was just the candlelight, Georgie.'

'But . . .'

She'd seen someone. Not clearly enough to make out their features, but there had been a person standing there.

'Hey, hey.' He rubbed her arm gently. 'It's okay. Nothing to worry about. If it *was* a burglar,' and there was a grin in

43

his voice now, 'they must have seen they were interrupting a special moment and left us to it.'

Georgina was so far from finding this funny.

Bren put a hand on her leg. Was he actually expecting to pick up where they had left off? She stood up abruptly.

'I'm going to check the front of the house,' she said. 'Would you blow out the candles, please? They're freaking me out.'

Leaving Bren to his disappointment, she marched off to look out the front window.

The street was still. Deserted. The flowerbeds and parked cars all moonlit with a silver glow.

That night, Georgina lay awake long after Bren began to snore. Listening to the creaks of the house. The pipes in the walls. The far-off shriek of a fox screaming somewhere in the night. It took her a long time to fall asleep.

8

The table was scattered with the debris of a family morning –
coffee-stained mugs, crumbs, a half-eaten bowl of cereal.
The book Cody had been reading lay face down on Bren's
newspaper, abandoned in the Monday rush to school.

Usually Georgina used the mornings to catch up on college
work. But today she hadn't been able to concentrate. Now she
simply sat there nursing a cup of chamomile tea as it turned cold.

The figure at the window was still vivid in her mind.

'There was nobody there, Georgina.' By the broad light
of day, Bren's assertions had sounded far more convincing.
Intellectually, Georgina knew he was right, and when Bren
and Cody were filling the house with chatter, it was easy to
believe it in her bones.

But when she found herself at home alone, her bones
weren't so sure.

A bird fluttered in the garden, black wings flapping, and
Georgina's head jerked around sharply.

Stop it, she told herself firmly. She'd been spooked by Cody's stories, that was all. She wouldn't have overreacted like that on Saturday night if the memory of him giggling on the phone hadn't been so fresh in her mind.

If there was just some way to put the matter to rest, once and for all . . .

After a moment's thought, she picked up her mobile, googled the customer service number for their phone provider and called it.

'Hi,' she said to the smooth-voiced adviser, who introduced herself as Nina. 'I was wondering if you could post me out a record of all incoming calls to my landline.'

'Your handset will keep a record of all incoming calls, ma'am,' said Nina. When Georgina explained that her house phone was so dated it did not, in fact, do this, Nina replied with a touch of impatience: 'Well then I suggest upgrading to a modern handset. Telecom companies don't provide customers with a log of inbound calls.'

'Please,' said Georgina. 'The information must be in your computer system somewhere, right? I just need to see who's been calling my landline. I realise this is unusual, but it's to do with my son. I just want to make sure he's safe.'

There was a pause. When the woman spoke again, it was in a different voice.

'I'm sorry. But you'd need a court order or a warrant to access those records.'

'But,' said Georgina hopefully, 'if the information is there, couldn't *you* find it and send it to me?'

'I'm sorry,' said Nina again, and she sounded like she meant it. 'I can't. But if a child is at risk, perhaps you're in a position to get a court order.'

For a brief moment, Georgina imagined trying to explain the situation to a judge.

'Hello?' said Nina. 'Are you still there?'

Suddenly embarrassed, Georgina thanked Nina for her time and ended the call. She stood up, threw the dregs of her tea down the sink and set about tidying the kitchen.

It was a relief to leave for work. The morning was bright, the street busy. The Brazilian couple from number 24 walked past, hand-in-hand, beaming, the woman's free hand resting on her bump. Georgina wondered where they were off to – the hospital for a scan, perhaps? They looked far too happy to be going to work.

Grey-haired, broad-shouldered Anthony from next door was also on his way to start the day.

'Morning, Georgina.'

'Morning, Anthony.'

Anthony could be grouchy, but on a good day you could get him to soften up. When he softened up, he sometimes stopped to chat, usually about his granddaughter, Lily, whom he adored. Georgina had heard a lot about Lily (seven years old, same as Cody, loved school, wanted to be a pirate when she grew up). Anthony had a tendency to go on and on once he'd started, and today Georgina hoped to escape his small talk.

'How're you getting on, Georgina? How's your little fella?'

Anthony only ever asked about Cody as a method of segueing Lily into the conversation.

'He's good, Anthony, thanks.'

'Yeah? That's great. Lily's doing great too. She got top marks in her spelling test, d'you know that? Knows how to spell all these words, long words, at her age! She's bright as a button . . .'

47

Then followed a dull litany of long words Lily could spell. Georgina nodded along politely, her mind elsewhere.

As he grew enthused, Anthony gesticulated, and that was what drew Georgina's attention to his injury.

'Anthony! Your hand!'

On his right hand were several deep red gouges.

He looked down and chuckled. 'Oh, that,' he said, taking a pair of black gloves out of his pocket and pulling them on.

'What happened?' Georgina asked.

'You wouldn't believe me.'

'Try me.' She was intrigued.

Anthony paused, a twinkle in his pale blue eyes.

'It was my pet rabbit.'

'Your *rabbit*?' Gruff, burly Anthony was the last person she would have expected to have a fluffy pet.

'I know,' he said wryly. 'I bought her for Lily, for Christmas. Lily's all excited, right? Brilliant! A rabbit! I was the best grandad in the whole world – for five minutes. Because what does the bleedin' thing do when I pick it up to give it to her? Bites me. Hard. First thing Christmas morning.'

Georgina began to laugh. Anthony was grinning too, shaking his head.

'Didn't realise rabbits could give you such a bite,' he said, warming to his story. 'But this one's vicious, right? Blood goes everywhere. Lily's bawling. "I don't want a rabbit any more, Granda," she says. "I don't like the rabbit, take her away." So that's it. I'm stuck with the bleedin' rabbit now.'

He gave his head another rueful shake, then glanced at his watch. 'I better run, Georgina. I've to go pick my ma up at the hospital.'

My ma.

48

Those two small words hit Georgina like a punch to the gut.

'Oh,' she managed to say. 'I hope it's nothing serious.'

'Just a routine thing,' said Anthony. 'She'll be grand. I better leg it. Catch you later, Georgina.'

He walked off, leaving Georgina reeling. Anthony must be pushing sixty, but he still had his mother. Thirty years older than she was and he could still refer casually to his ma like a little boy. Would she even remember Rose's voice by the time she reached his age?

The wave of grief blindsided her. She stumbled to the car, got in, put her head on the steering wheel and sobbed.

During every difficult period in Georgina's life, her mother had been by her side, unfailingly frank, funny and forthright. 'You can't fall apart now,' she'd told her during those dark months after Cody's birth. 'Mothers don't have the luxury of falling apart. There's too much bleedin' housework to be done.' Rose had been the kind of person you could always depend on to answer the phone. How impossible it seemed that that number didn't call any more.

When the tears subsided a little, Georgina sat up. She had to pull herself together. She had work.

As her mother always told her: focus on the small things, one at a time.

She checked her make-up in the rear-view mirror, wiping the mascara smudges from under her eyes. Taking several deep breaths, she turned the key in the ignition and set off for work.

9

'Georgina. *Georgina.*'

She jolted upright to find herself at the kitchen table, laptop and notes spread around her.

'You were asleep,' said Bren.

'What time is it?'

'Seven a.m.'

There was a small patch of saliva on the page in front of her. Georgina groaned. She must have fallen asleep within minutes of making her way downstairs at five a.m. Dammit. She'd missed out on a whole two hours of study time.

The rest of the day dragged. Georgina yawned her way through her shift at the bookshop. She collected Cody from the after-school club he attended on the days she worked full shifts, took him grocery shopping and then went home to cook dinner.

It was half past six before she finally got to sit down and open her laptop again. She was determined to use these last days of the Christmas break to catch up on college work. To prove the little voice in her head wrong. The one that whispered: *You'll drop out again. You're not able for it.*

Georgina had been in her second year of art college when the panic attacks and depression she was struggling with became too much. The loss of the college course she'd loved had been with her since – that and the sense of failure. Gathering the courage to go back had taken many years and a lot of encouragement from Bren. She had to stay on top of things this time around. She *had* to.

After a solid hour's studying, the knot in her stomach had eased somewhat. She was able to relax during dinner. They ate as a family, around the kitchen table, in the warm light of the crooked lamp. Happy and laughing. Bren opened a bottle of wine. The fiasco on Saturday night, the figure at the window, seemed far away, silly. A trick of the light, like Bren had said.

After dinner, Bren cleared up, allowing Georgina to go back to her studies. By the time they were undressing for bed, she felt more relaxed than she had in a long time.

Bren pulled his T-shirt off. Georgina, sitting on the side of the bed, watched him. He'd been going to the gym a lot lately. He looked good. She wished she could convert her objective appreciation of this fact into a more sexual response.

Try, she told herself. As he walked around in his jeans, Georgina tried to see him with fresh eyes, as if she were a new lover sitting on the side of his bed for the first time.

Bren caught her staring. 'What?' he said with amusement.

She met his gaze without speaking. They looked at each other steadily, and the atmosphere of the room changed.

'Come here,' she said.

Wordless, he walked over and stood in front of her. She leant forward, kissing his bare skin. At his sharp intake of breath, she felt the beginnings of real arousal inside her – tempered by uncertainty.

Did she want to do this? She wasn't sure.

She stood up.

'Where are you going?' He looked schoolboy-hopeful.

'I'll be back in a minute.'

In the bathroom, she looked at herself in the mirror. *Try.* As she brushed her teeth, she imagined finishing what they had started on Saturday night. Her desire felt like an elusive bird that had chosen to perch on her shoulder. Now that it was there, she had to be cautious, mindful not to let it flutter away. She tried to stay focused on the pulse of excitement that had moved through her and settled in her lower body when Bren's breathing changed . . .

It was then that she heard something. A strange scraping noise in the back garden.

The bathroom window was textured glass. Georgina opened it to look outside. Cold night air blew in. Had she imagined the sound?

No. There it was again. Louder, now that the window was open.

A steady *scrape . . . scrape . . . scrape.*

Their back garden was small enough to take in at a glance, and it was deserted. So unless the noise was coming from their side gate . . .

Then she saw something moving.

Not in their garden. In Anthony's.

It took Georgina's brain several seconds to understand what she was seeing.

There was somebody standing behind Anthony's shed, holding a long implement. A stick? They were moving it rhythmically. *Scrape . . . scrape . . . scrape.*

Then she realised the scraping sound was a shovel in the earth.

The person was *digging*.

Her eyes, adjusting to the dark, made out grey hair, broad shoulders . . .

It was Anthony himself.

No longer frightened, but utterly fascinated, Georgina watched him for a moment. What on earth was he doing?

Then she remembered that Bren was waiting for her and guiltily pulled the window shut, hurrying back to the bedroom.

When she described the scene to Bren, he seemed amused. 'What an oddball. Neighbours, eh?' He slid his arms around her waist. 'What d'you reckon, Georgie? Bit of midnight gardening? Or maybe he's burying a body?'

His lips brushed her neck. She could tell he didn't really care what oddities the neighbours were up to.

'It's so strange,' she said, whispering now. 'Don't you want to see for yourself?'

'Honestly,' said Bren, pulling her a little closer, 'no.'

His mouth was moving down to her collarbone now in a way that was particularly distracting.

'I'll get the lights,' she said.

They got under the covers. At first, it was almost awkward, trying to find each other's faces in the dark.

Then, suddenly, it wasn't.

Bren pressed against her and her body began to melt. Her hips pushed up to meet his. She could feel herself falling into that headspace where she could think of nothing else.

Is he thinking about Emma right now? Does he ever think about Emma when we do this?

The unwanted thought came out of nowhere.

'Something wrong?' Bren asked.

'Nothing's wrong.' She tried to force the image of Emma's green eyes out of her mind. *Let it go, Georgina, for God's sake.* 'I'm fine.'

Willing it to be true, she kissed him hard – but now she found she was faking. The flow had been broken. Bren, still lost in the moment, groaned against her neck. Eyes closed, she tried to get back to where she had been . . .

The shadows. The clock. The stuffed toy.

She broke away from Bren, heart pounding. Why would she think about that *now*?

'What's the matter?'

'I'm fine.' She couldn't articulate it, even if she had wanted to. 'I just . . . can't get in the mood for some reason. I'm sorry.'

'That's all right,' said Bren, perfectly evenly. 'It's okay, Georgina.'

But if his secret thought was *You can never get in the mood these days*, Georgina could hardly have blamed him. The room seemed empty without his boyish excitement of a moment ago.

'I'm sorry,' she said. 'I just feel . . . '

What did she feel?

'Georgina,' Bren said with more emphasis, 'it's *okay*.'

He sounded like he meant it, but the shapes their bodies made beside each other were awkward that night, and it made her feel painfully lonely. Why was her subconscious sending her these memories? To sabotage the moment? Maybe on some level she didn't want to save her marriage. What is wrong with me? she wondered.

IO

'Vera,' said Georgina, 'how long were you and Frank married for?'

Her afternoon studying had been interrupted by a rapping at the window. She'd looked up to see Vera's round face peering in at her. Now the two women were sitting at Georgina's kitchen table, sharing tea and cake and stories.

Since Vera's family had moved away, Georgina always tried to make time for her, and on this occasion she was glad of the distraction from her books. She'd been having trouble concentrating. Her unsuccessful attempt to reconnect with Bren kept flashing across her mind.

Of course, it didn't hurt that Vera had brought over a Tupperware box full of freshly baked brownies.

'Frank and me were married thirty-six years.' Vera sat back comfortably as Georgina poured her a fresh cup of tea. 'We were two months shy of our thirty-sixth anniversary when he had the heart attack, but I always count the thirty-six.'

'Wow,' said Georgina, daunted by the thought of such a huge stretch of time.

'Thirty-six years, and he was gone just like that,' Vera said, shaking her head. 'I was in the garden – two sugars, please, Georgina – and I heard a terrible shout. I went rushing in, and there he was on the floor.'

'Jesus. That's awful.'

'A normal Saturday morning, and by the afternoon I had no husband. You never know which day will be the one that changes your life.'

Vera spoke quite cheerfully, but Georgina, not exactly heartened by this gloomy proclamation, moved back to the original topic.

'What would you say is the secret to a happy marriage?'

'Oh now. Let me think.' Vera clasped her fresh cup of tea in both hands, clearly enjoying herself. 'Appreciation,' she said. 'And affection. Make it a habit in your marriage to show each other appreciation and affection every day.'

Georgina immediately began to worry about the levels of appreciation and affection in her own marriage.

'If you're about to start an argument with your husband,' Vera continued, 'ask yourself first if you're hungry or tired.'

'Okay,' Georgina smiled, picking up her half-eaten brownie, 'that's pretty spot on. Half the time Bren and I get snippy with each other, it's lack of sleep.'

Vera pushed her owlish glasses up her nose. 'And have lots of sex,' she added.

Georgina choked on a bite of brownie.

'Well, it's very important in a relationship.' Vera grinned wickedly at her. 'Young people nowadays are always talking about it – well I hope you're all *doing* it half as much as you talk about it.'

Georgina was still laughing, but inside she winced. If Vera knew how close to home that one had landed . . .

After Vera left, Georgina cleared the table and returned to studying until an alarm reminded her it was time to collect Cody from school. On the drive there, she mulled over Vera's advice. *Appreciation. Affection.* She tried, didn't she? *Have lots of sex . . .*

Georgina parked and joined the other parents at the school gates. *How much sex d'you think she's having?* she couldn't help wondering when another mother waved at her. *How about her over there?*

She was distracted when Cody appeared carrying a shapeless papier-mâché creation.

'Wow, Cody. That's really . . . something.' She couldn't guess what it was supposed to be.

'It's Dad,' he supplied helpfully. 'Look, the cotton wool is his hair.'

Georgina hid her smile. 'Ah,' she said. 'Yes. I see it now.'

In the car home, Cody kept up a monologue about his artwork. 'The pasta is teeth,' he explained. 'And I didn't know how to do ears, so he doesn't have ears.'

Georgina made vague sounds of interest, trying to seem like an engaged, involved parent.

'Mam. You're not *looking*.'

'I'm trying to drive, Cody. I'm looking as best I can, okay?'

By the time they reached their street, Cody had moved on to detailing a plan he and Patrick had hatched to sabotage Team Purple's star chart and prevent them from winning the weekly lollipops. Half amused, half wondering how serious this plot was and whether she should intervene, Georgina was distracted, and Cody noticed before she did.

'What's that, Mam?'

Something was strewn across their driveway.

'Mam, it's your plants!'

Georgina jerkily pulled the car in on the road outside the house.

'Wait here, sweetie.'

She jumped out. Cody was right. It was her plants. The pots that flanked the front door, the hanging baskets, they'd all been smashed to pieces. Broken ceramic and scattered soil littered the concrete.

'Oh God.'

She crouched down to inspect the debris. The petals she'd chosen for their winter bloom were shredded and destroyed, stamped into pulp.

'Who did this, Mam?'

Cody, ignoring her warning, had followed her out of the car.

'I don't know,' Georgina said, straightening up. But as she stood among the ruins of her flowers, she saw again the image of the figure at the window.

'Maybe it was a ghost,' Cody suggested.

'Maybe,' she replied, striving to keep her tone light. 'Let's go inside, shall we? It's cold.'

Cody poked at the ceramic shards with a toe.

'Cody. Come on.'

But he didn't move. He was looking down at the broken pots thoughtfully.

'Maybe it was New Granny,' he said.

Georgina struggled to hide the flutter of fear she felt at those words.

'Why do you say that, Cody?'

'Because she's angry at you.'

Georgina glanced around the street. All she saw was a stooped old man she didn't recognise, walking a dog. And a crow, cawing and flapping its wings in a nearby tree.

'Why would New Granny be angry at me, Cody?' she asked, moving him towards the house. She wanted badly to be inside. To put the solid weight of the front door between herself and the street.

Cody shrugged. 'I think because you said I shouldn't take sweets off her.'

The crow cawed again, jostling the dead, leafless branches of the tree as it took flight.

'Inside, Cody,' said Georgina sharply. '*Now.*'

11

Georgina felt on edge all afternoon at home by herself with Cody. The broken pots and soil remained scattered across the driveway. Georgina didn't want to go out there to sweep up. Not alone. Not with dusk rapidly descending.

Even in the cheerfully cluttered rooms of her house, in the yellow glow of the crooked lamp, she couldn't relax. Shadows seemed darker than usual. Her nervousness lent an unfamiliar edge to her own home. When she heard Bren's key in the door, she jumped up in relief.

'What the hell happened to your plants?' was his first question.

Georgina glanced meaningfully into the front room, where Cody was engrossed in a game on the iPad. She beckoned Bren to the kitchen, where, on the sofa in the corner, she told him everything, ending with what Cody had said.

She felt shivery when she'd finished, and perhaps Bren noticed, because he took the knitted blanket from the back of the sofa and wrapped it around her shoulders.

'Don't worry about it,' he said comfortingly. 'We can buy new hanging baskets. It's not that big a deal.'

Georgina felt like they'd gone offtrack. 'I know we can replace the pots. What I'm wondering is – who broke them?'

Bren frowned. 'What d'you mean? Georgina, this is Dublin. Random vandalism happens.'

'You really think this is random? What about what Cody said?'

'Of course it is. Look, I'll have a chat with Cody. Maybe that was his way of saying he's angry at us for not taking his game more seriously.'

'Bren, you didn't hear him. The way he said it . . . it was creepy.'

Bren looked thoughtful. 'All right then,' he said in a reasonable voice. 'What's your theory?'

'What?'

'Who do you think broke the pots? What exactly do you think is happening?'

'What exactly? I don't know.' Georgina pulled the blanket tighter around herself, feeling ridiculously put on the spot. 'I just think that maybe something . . . strange is going on,' she finished lamely.

Bren let that hang in the air between them.

'Look, I don't have a theory,' she admitted. 'But . . . Cody's game. The person I thought I saw. And now this. Aren't you worried it might all be connected?'

'Of course not.' Bren began to stroke her back. 'There's no logical reason for it to be. Look, I'll talk to Cody. But we have to let him—'

'Grieve in his own way. I know.' Georgina closed her eyes.

'It's a shame about your plants, Georgie. But it's just one of those unfortunate things. It's not worth getting upset over.'

He was still rubbing circles between her shoulder blades. Moving away, Georgina opened her eyes – and noticed the time.

'God, I almost forgot!' She got to her feet. 'I told my dad I'd go around this evening and help him with those boxes. I'm going to be late.'

She paused. The thought of leaving Cody now made her uneasy. But that was silly, of course. Bren was here.

'I'll sweep up the garden,' he said. 'You go.'

'Thanks,' said Georgina, pulling on her coat. 'There's some of that curry left in the fridge for dinner.'

'Do you want us to save you some?'

'Don't worry about it. You know my dad. He'll probably insist on ordering pizza.'

As she left the house, Georgina tried not to look down at the broken pots.

Maybe it was New Granny.

But on the drive to her father's house, she couldn't get the image of them out of her head.

She's angry at you.

'You all right, love?' Jimmy asked when she got there. 'You seem a bit off.'

'What? No. I'm grand.'

'D'you want a bite to eat before we get started?' Instead of going upstairs, where the boxes of his late wife's things were waiting, Jimmy headed for the kitchen. 'I'm going to make myself a sandwich.'

Georgina had predicted her father would invent reasons to procrastinate.

'You have one, Dad,' she said gently. 'I'll head up and start.'

She walked upstairs alone, mind drifting back to her conversation with Bren.

Random vandalism . . . Not worth getting upset over . . .

Was Bren right? Was it just a string of unsettling coincidences? That must be it, she told herself. After all, what else could it be? The broken pots had unnerved her because being the victim of any crime, even petty vandalism, was upsetting. It was natural that she'd been shaken. Especially on top of Cody acting so strangely . . .

She reached the cluttered hall and took a deep breath. Right. She had a job to do.

She knelt down on the carpet, opened the nearest box and tried to focus on the task at hand: unpacking and folding her mother's old clothes. She took out a beautiful lace dress. A pair of velvet shoes. A hounds-tooth coat Rose had worn a lot last winter – her last Christmas.

She took out her phone and pulled up the photos. Herself and her mother standing outside a Dublin restaurant in their winter coats, arm-in-arm, eyes crinkled with laughter.

'Georgina?' Jimmy called from downstairs. 'You sure you don't want that sandwich, love?'

'I'm fine,' she called back.

She put her phone away and kept sorting. A pair of elegant silver earrings. A woollen jacket.

And then, among the clothes, she found a framed photograph. Taken at a party, decades ago. Her parents looked to be in their thirties. They were laughing with her uncle Billy, heads thrown back. Rose, holding a champagne glass and wearing a fitted black dress, wouldn't have looked out of place alongside the Hollywood starlets of the film noir days. And Billy, clearly recognisable by his prominent nose and ears, must have only been twenty-five or so. Face smooth, shoulders broad and strong. It was jarring to see him like that – a man who'd been turned slow and senile by early-onset Alzheimer's, who barely recognised visitors to his nursing home any more.

Georgina felt, like a physical ache, an awareness of the passing of time. Her parents and Billy had been like this once. Vibrantly alive. Now Rose was gone, Jimmy was alone, Billy was wasting away in a home . . .

She began to cry, big tears rolling down her nose.

'Georgina.' Jimmy's footsteps creaked on the stairs. 'I brought you up a sandwich just in case you changed your . . . Georgina, are you crying?'

Leaving the sandwich by the top of the stairs, he hurried over as fast as his legs would allow. Georgina got to her feet clumsily. The confusion and panic she'd felt over these past days, the unrelenting ache of grief in her chest . . . it was all released in huge, uncontrollable sobs.

Her father put a big arm around her shoulders and hugged her tight. 'What's the matter, love?'

She wiped her nose and sniffed. She wanted to say *I miss Mam*, but she didn't think she could handle it if Jimmy crumbled too, not at this very moment. She was still holding the photo.

'I feel bad that I don't visit Billy more often.' That might not be the deepest reason for her tears, but it was true, and just saying it made her feel weepy again.

'Ah Georgina.' Jimmy's arm tightened around her. 'I've told you not to feel bad about that. I'm the only person Billy remembers now. He just gets confused by other visitors.'

'I know, but . . . I still feel awful that I don't see him more often.' Georgina had never been that close to Billy, but had felt an obligation to visit him nonetheless. However, after Rose's diagnosis, other obligations had seemed to fall away. 'I'm a bad niece,' she said, and with those words she began to bawl again.

'You're not, Georgina,' said her father, 'not at all! Shush now. You're a great girl.'

But the tears kept coming. It wasn't just Billy. It was Cody's strange game, and the shock of the broken pots earlier, and how exhausted she felt every day, and ...

'I miss Mam.' As soon as the words blurted out, she was glad she'd said them. 'I miss her so much.'

'Oh Georgie.' Jimmy hugged her hard against his chest. They stood like that for a while. 'I miss her too. Every minute of every day.'

When her tears had dried, Jimmy helped her move the remaining boxes into the spare room. She'd leave the rest until another day.

'Will you hang around and watch a bit of telly, Georgina?'

'Course.'

'We might as well order some food, mightn't we? How about pizza?'

She had to smile.

'Go on then.'

As she put the photograph away, she felt tears threaten once more. *I should go visit Billy soon, never mind what Dad says.* When she had the time.

Despite it all, they went on to have an enjoyable evening. The pizza arrived. Georgina and Jimmy had their requisite argument about what to watch. Jimmy liked his movies solidly entertaining (Bren had long since learnt that suggesting documentaries was a lost cause), and Georgina's suggestion of *The Magdalene Sisters* was shot down immediately as being too depressing – Jimmy's most common criticism of art.

'If I wanted to be depressed, Georgina, I'd read a newspaper. Put on *Point Break* instead.'

Point Break was Jimmy's favourite film. Georgina had seen it more times than she cared to count. Resigned, she settled on the sofa to watch two hours of Keanu Reeves running around on a beach, and found it strangely comforting.

12

It was that slice of morning peace Georgina enjoyed on the days she wasn't in work till ten. Bren and Cody had left for the school run. Having already fitted in an hour and a half of studying before breakfast, she was using this silent time to tidy the kitchen and put away laundry. It felt like a luxury to do chores without interruption.

As she carried a basketful of clothes to Cody's room, her soft steps on the carpet were the only sound in the house.

Cody's bedroom was small and colourful, painted a bright, happy yellow. Every surface was cluttered with books, half-finished science experiments, and toys that were much loved one week and forgotten the next. His drawings were tacked all over the walls. In one corner stood the 'fort' he had constructed with a red blanket, an old broom handle and Bren's help. A crumpled piece of paper bearing the warning CODY'S FORT – KEEP OUT was taped over the entrance.

Georgina picked her way over the pencils and open sketchbooks scattered across the carpet to put the laundry basket down on the unmade bed. God, this place was a mess. She set about clearing the floor before she tripped over something.

One of Cody's sketchbooks was open at a drawing of Georgina. She picked up the book and sat down on her son's bed, smiling at his crayon-and-pencil impression of her. He always used a bright yellow scribble for her fair hair, and he always drew her smiling, a huge, wobbly but determined black line curving across the stick-woman's face.

Wishing she could hug him right now, Georgina turned the page.

The next picture was of Cody. She recognised the way he drew himself, too: black crayon for hair, his favourite red shoes coloured in. But he wasn't alone.

Stick-figure Cody was holding hands with a stick-figure old woman.

The smile faded from Georgina's face. She remembered Bren's protestations. *Just a game . . . His way of feeling close to Rose . . .*

The old woman in the picture had a scribble of short grey hair. Rose McGrath had dyed her hair vivid red until the day she died.

Heart beating faster, Georgina turned another page. The grey-haired woman again, with trees and swings beside her. The park.

In the next drawing, the stick-figure grandmother had her stick-arms stretched out as if for a hug. Cody had written underneath, in his childish letters: *New Granny.*

The coldness spreading through Georgina went right down to her bones. She was frozen where she sat. Too afraid to look around. Afraid she would see a face pressed against the window, staring in at . . .

Stop it.

She closed the sketchbook and forced herself to take a deep, calming breath. She was on the first floor. Nobody could be looking in. She glanced over her shoulder. Daylight was streaming through the window. She was safe.

Resolved, she began to search Cody's bedroom. She didn't know what she was looking for exactly, and her search turned up nothing. In frustration, she paced the carpet. *Think. THINK.*

Some of the clothes Cody wore more often, his coats and hoodies, hung on the hallstand downstairs.

Taking the steps two at a time, she hurried down to rifle through the pockets. She turned out a broken pencil, a rubber frog, some stray plastic penguin and monkey bullets . . . And then, in the inside pocket of his green raincoat, her fingers touched something that crinkled.

She pulled out a handful of golden toffee wrappers.

Georgina blinked at them. A memory was tugging at her. She pulled the plastic taut and read the words CAFFREY'S CONFECTIONERY.

Then it came back to her.

For a moment, she was back in the bushes in the park, surrounded by the rustling leaves, tugging a wrapper from the dirt.

Georgina felt a fear like she had never known rising through her. Even when she'd seen the drawings, some part of her hadn't quite believed there was anything going on.

But this – the same sweet wrappers from the park, now in Cody's pocket . . .

She closed her eyes briefly, trying to hold herself together. *Mothers don't have the luxury of falling apart.*

Hands trembling, she went downstairs and located her phone. She tapped the words *Caffrey's Confectionery* into Google and clicked Search.

A website appeared:

Welcome to CAFFREY'S CONFECTIONERY
Purveyors of classic sweets since 1924

Georgina read on shakily.

We are a small, family-run business.
Shop online here!
Our products can also be bought at these outlets:

There followed a list of places where the toffees could be purchased. Georgina recognised only two of the locations: Conkers Café in Rathmines and Healthy Green, the hipster supermarket in Smithfield. The sort of places that stocked pricey, artisanal products.

Even Bren would have to see that this couldn't be a coincidence. Someone had given Cody those sweets.

And that person had been in the bushes that day in the park. Standing just a few feet away from Georgina, watching her from the shadows as her 'Hello?' fell flat on the frosty grass.

Georgina stood up sharply. She wanted to get out of the house. But she already knew her hours at work would be spent mentally fast-forwarding to the moment she could show Bren what she had found. Solid evidence that this wasn't all in Cody's – or Georgina's – head. Something undeniable, something material, something she could hold in her hand.

13

The sketchbook was open on the kitchen table. Beside it lay the handful of golden wrappers. Bren stood leafing through the pages, looking at each drawing but making no comment. Georgina hovered nearby, waiting anxiously for his verdict.

'Well these are certainly creepy,' he said eventually. 'I get why you were upset. But they don't prove anything other than what we already know – Cody has an imaginary grandmother.'

Georgina was at a loss. She had been certain that when she showed him this evidence, he'd be on her side. That they'd take steps together to protect Cody.

'But you said this game was his way of mourning Rose. That's clearly not a drawing of my mother.'

Bren shrugged. 'So he dreamt up a more generic grandmother. One who looks like the grandparents his friends have, or the ones he sees in books.'

He closed the sketchpad and stepped away from the table, looking at Georgina with finality.

'But the wrappers.' She gestured towards them. 'They're a speciality brand. Hard to find. It's proof.'

'Proof of what? That Cody ate some sweets?'

Georgina didn't like the way Bren was looking at her.

'That there was really someone there,' she answered hesitantly. 'In the park that day. The same person who's been giving Cody these fancy sweets.' That was obvious – wasn't it?

Bren was silent.

'Bren,' Georgina went on, desperate now, 'please listen to me. I think someone's in contact with our son. We'd be bad parents if we didn't take this seriously.'

Bren didn't speak for a while. He rubbed his face with one hand, scratching at several days' growth of stubble. Then he said evenly, 'That's not fair, Georgina. I'm not a bad parent because I won't join in your delusion.'

'*What?*' The word gasped out of her.

'Oh, you can imply that I'm a bad parent, but I can't point out how fucking *insane* this is?'

Georgina flinched. Bren looked immediately contrite.

'Sorry, Georgie. I didn't mean it to come out like that. I'm just worried about you.'

'I'm fine.' Well, maybe not *fine* exactly, but ... 'It's Cody we should be worried about.'

Bren continued as if she hadn't spoken. 'I've been worried about you for a while, Georgina. You've been under so much strain lately. You're not coping.'

And before she could collect her thoughts, he'd unzipped his backpack and produced a leaflet.

'I hate to bring this up during a row, but . . . ' He handed it to her. 'I really do think you should go and speak to someone.'

Georgina stared down at the leaflet. The front featured a pretty blonde woman holding a cup of tea and staring into the distance, wearing a vacant expression apparently intended to look pensive. The bright blue text read: *Want to take steps to a healthier, happier, less stressed you? Don't know where to begin? Take the first step by calling Better Steps Therapy today.*

'I've done my research,' said Bren. 'This place is supposed to be really excellent. I think therapy could really—'

'I don't need therapy!' Georgina burst out. 'I don't need to take steps to a less stressed me!' She grabbed the handful of toffee wrappers off the table. 'I didn't imagine these! Someone's giving Cody sweets! It's this old woman . . . She's *real*. Bren, you have to believe me.'

Bren's face was a mask of pity and concern.

'Oh Georgie,' was all he said.

Georgina's fingers closed tight on the toffee wrappers. How could she make him see? She stood there for a long moment, staring at the vacuous model on the front of the counselling leaflet, brain whirring.

Then the answer clicked in her mind. It was so simple, so obvious.

'Let's ask Cody.'

'What?'

'Let's ask him! He's been telling us all along that this woman is real, and we haven't been listening to him. Let's listen.'

Bren looked thoughtful. 'All right,' he said. 'It might be good for you. But let me do the talking, okay?'

Georgina shoved the wrappers into her pocket.

'Okay.'

Cody was lying on his bed, reading, when they entered his room.

'Hey, buddy.' Bren sat down on the edge of the bed. Georgina lingered nervously by the door.

Cody observed his parents with a tinge of alarm. Georgina guessed he was going over his many small crimes in his head, wondering which he had been caught out for. She felt a rush of love for her mischievous son.

'It's all right, kiddo,' said Bren. 'You're not in trouble.' Cody visibly relaxed. 'We just want to ask you a few questions.'

It sounds like a police interview, Georgina thought.

'It's about New Granny,' said Bren. 'You know that game you've been playing, buddy?'

Was it Georgina's imagination, or did Cody tense up?

'Well, we have a question, and the answer is important.' Bren was using the kind, measured tones that Georgina always admired in his parenting. 'We know New Granny is real to you, but we want to know: is she *real* real? I know you can see her, but is she a person me and Mam would be able to see?'

Cody took his time answering. He looked at both his parents thoughtfully, his eyes moving across his father's face, then his mother's.

'No,' he said. 'I made her up.'

Bren looked over at Georgina. *There you go*, his expression said.

Georgina kept her gaze trained on her son. 'You made her up, Cody?'

'Yes.' His voice was clear and innocent. 'It was a game.'

'Then where did these come from?' She produced the handful of golden toffee wrappers. 'New Granny gave them to you, didn't she?'

75

Cody hesitated, looking trapped. Bren was frowning at Georgina, but she ignored him.

'Was it New Granny?' she repeated with more force. 'Tell the truth!'

'Jesus, Georgina.' Bren stood up. 'They're sweets. He could have got them anywhere. From a party, from a friend at school . . .'

Cody was listening intently from the bed.

'Yeah,' he piped up. 'I got them from my friend at school.'

His eyes were huge and blue. Georgina looked directly into them. 'Which friend, Cody?'

'Umm . . . I forget.'

'Cody, tell me which friend.'

'Georgina, *stop it*.' Bren's tone was absolute, and Georgina, not wanting to enter into a full-on row in front of Cody, allowed herself to be ushered out of the room. As they left, she glanced back at her son. That wide-eyed expression was one he often wore when telling a lie.

14

I made her up.

I made her up.

Throughout the following day – at work, during the school run – those words echoed in Georgina's head.

I made her up.

She tried to question Cody after school, but 'I told you already. Leave me *alone*' was all he would say, turning his face stubbornly away from her. Then Bren came home from work early, and she knew her chance was gone.

'How are you feeling?' Bren kept speaking to her in a Very Kind voice, the way the young speak to the elderly and infirm. 'Have you had a chance to think about what I said? I can call up the counselling service and make an appointment for you if you'd like.'

Georgina knew he meant well, patronising as he was. But she refused to be talked around any more. All along, Cody's game had given Georgina the same feeling a spider's wriggling black legs gave her – a crawling sensation along her skin.

It was Bren who had convinced her not to take that feeling seriously. Bren, in his unshakeable belief that his own logic was infallible.

She should have listened to her gut from the beginning.

'Georgina? Did you get a chance to read that leaflet?'

She mumbled something about needing fresh air. She grabbed her coat and scarf, dodged past her husband and slipped out.

But she didn't go for a walk. Instead, she went around to the side of her house and looked at the side gate. She remembered the figure at the window last Saturday. The one Bren had been so certain was a trick of the light.

Was it plausible that somebody had jumped over this gate? Was Cody's new friend watching their family?

Georgina stared at the side gate, wondering how easy it was to climb.

Only one way to find out.

She stepped onto the low wall that separated their garden from Anthony's and heaved herself up and over the gate, landing comfortably in the back garden.

It wasn't difficult at all. Any able-bodied person could do that.

In fact, she realised, if somebody stood on the wall, reached over and undid the bolt, they'd be able to walk straight through. No vaulting necessary.

As she stood there in the dark and cold, contemplating this unpleasant fact, Georgina felt eyes on her. She turned her gaze upwards and saw that Anthony was watching her from an upstairs window. They made eye contact, and he stepped quickly out of sight.

Odd man, Georgina thought, remembering his midnight digging behind the shed. But then, she conceded, *she* was the eccentric neighbour now, wasn't she? Anthony must think she was loopy, jumping over her own side gate . . .

Standing exactly where the person had stood on that night, Georgina looked in her kitchen window. Had they been trying to scare her? Or hoping to go unnoticed?

Bren was in the front room with Cody. There was no one to see her looking around the garden, using the torch on her phone. She wasn't sure what she was looking *for*, exactly. Some clue, as if from a murder mystery novel? Footprints? A scrap of torn clothing? But she found nothing.

Their cramped little garden didn't take long to search. There was the single dogwood tree, the concrete paving, and a tiny shed that was usually locked. Without thinking, she tried the shed door and to her surprise found it open. Bren must have forgotten to lock it.

She stepped inside the shed, closing the door behind her.

It smelled damp and cold. By the light of her phone, Georgina could see cobwebs and clutter. Gardening shears. A shovel. Bren's hiking things – a backpack, walking poles, mud-caked boots – dumped out here, never cleaned. Just general domestic debris, but . . .

She confronted the fear that had been stirring in her subconscious since she realised the shed was unlocked. Someone could have hidden in here if they were watching the house.

The thought was ice water down her back.

She shone the torch around again. This time something caught her eye. A small object on the ground glittered green as it caught the light.

Georgina crouched down for a closer look. She reached through the clutter and pulled it free.

It was a green stone on a long gold chain. A necklace. By the torchlight, she stared at it. The stone was set in some ornate, rather fussy detail, the kind of thing she herself would never wear.

Perhaps it had belonged to some previous occupant of the house. That was certainly the most logical explanation. That was what Bren would say. *This house was built in 1922. Generations have lived and died here. It's hardly a great mystery, is it, Georgina?*

It did look old-fashioned. Like something from another era.

She shivered, slipped the necklace into her pocket and got out of the shed fast.

When Bren saw her back in the house, he did a double-take.

'Georgina. I didn't hear you come in.'

She shrugged. Was there any point explaining that she'd been in the shed or showing him the necklace? Initiating another painful conversation during which he refused to take her seriously? Perhaps she should wait until she could connect the dots and present him with a complete picture.

But she was bursting to talk it through with *someone*. So that night, when Cody was asleep and Bren was in the bathroom, Georgina decided to tell him.

She was sitting on the side of the bed, setting her alarm for 4.30 the next morning. She wanted to get up particularly early to make up for the studying she had missed in her agitated state today.

Bren came back into the room yawning, wearing only the worn tracksuit bottoms he slept in. His face, just washed, looked oddly vulnerable without his glasses.

'There's something I want to show you,' she said.

He put his glasses back on.

'What's up?'

She took the necklace out of her pocket and placed it on the duvet. In her head, she tried to construct a sentence that wouldn't have him immediately casting aspersions on her sanity. *I found this in our shed. It's not mine.* That seemed like an ordinary thing to say, but she knew he would hear, and respond to, what she was really saying: *Don't you think that's suspicious?* God, how had everything become so fraught with difficulty?

It occurred to her then that she had been quiet for a while and he hadn't spoken. It was most unlike Bren not to speak.

She looked up and saw his expression.

Georgina knew immediately that Bren had seen the necklace before. All the colour had drained from his face in a startling way, as though the brightness had been turned down on a screen. His jawline was taut and strained.

'Where did you get that?'

'I found it,' she said, alarmed. 'Why? What's wrong?'

In the long silence that followed her question, Georgina felt her alarm solidify into fear.

'Bren?' she said.

15

They remained still as statues – Georgina on the bed, Bren standing, the necklace on the duvet between them.

'Where did you find it?' he said.

'It was in our shed,' she replied, puzzled and frightened by the look on his face. 'I don't understand. Whose necklace is it, Bren?'

Bren lowered his head into his hands. He stayed like that for a long moment. When he straightened up, his expression was completely miserable.

'It's Emma's,' he whispered.

'Emma's?' Georgina repeated. And then, saying the words as they came into her mind, feeling like every idiot wife since the dawn of time but unable to stop herself: 'What's Emma's necklace doing in our shed?'

Bren looked pained and desperate. He stood there as if he couldn't think of anything to do but wait for her to figure it out.

Slowly, reluctantly, her mind put it together. Bren's hiking things were still in the shed, where he had thrown them after that trip. The hiking things he had not used since the weekend of his kiss with Emma. That brief drunken slip-up to which he had – so bravely! – confessed. How impressed she had been by his honesty! His integrity!

Emma's necklace had been in their shed because it had fallen out of Bren's bag. And Emma's necklace had ended up in Bren's bag because . . .

'You slept together.' Georgina heard her own voice, calm and factual, as if she was reporting on the weather. Interesting that she could sound like that when there was a roaring in her ears. 'People don't remove their jewellery to kiss. You slept together.'

She could see it. Emma unclasping her necklace. Putting it to the side, where it had slipped into Bren's backpack. Or perhaps Bren had undone the clasp while Emma held her long dark hair out of the way.

Suddenly Georgina couldn't breathe.

Bren was shaking his head frantically, but not as an attempt at denial. As an expression of anguish. Like he couldn't believe this was happening.

'It was just that one time, Georgina,' he said, voice desperate. 'You have to believe me. Just that one night, and I swear – *I swear* – I cut contact afterwards. I've never felt worse about anything. I couldn't bear the thought of . . . I didn't tell you everything because . . . Jesus, Georgina, I don't know what to say. I love you. I made one stupid fucking mistake. I love you.'

As he talked, Georgina looked down at the coiled golden chain, the dragon-green stone. She had thought the necklace odd, old-fashioned. Now she realised it was the exact kind of piece a woman with a colourful, offbeat sense of fashion might pick up in a vintage shop or flea market. A woman like Emma, with her glossy dark hair and eyes that same shade of vivid green.

There was no great mystery here, no intrigue.

This was the oldest, most predictable story in the world.

Georgina had never felt so foolish, or so small.

Back when Bren had first confessed to his 'drunken kiss', Georgina had spent hours scouring the internet for any detail she could find about Emma. It wasn't just photos she was looking for; it was *anything*. Any smidgen of information about Emma's life or personality.

Emma's social media use was limited, most of her accounts protected with stringent privacy settings, but this only made what few crumbs were available seem even more tantalising. A couple of profile pictures visible on Facebook. Some activity on a Twitter account Emma had used briefly back in 2009, which included such banalities as 'Starving!! Might order pad thai ... nom nom.'

Now, lying in bed alone at night, with Bren downstairs on the sofa, Georgina found herself rereading those old tweets like they were some magnum opus. She had no idea why it was so fascinating to know that Emma enjoyed Thai food, she just knew that it *was*. She wanted to know where Emma went and who with, what TV shows she watched, what books she cried at, what she talked to her friends about, and by the way, what had it meant to her when she slept with Georgina's husband?

She looked at the photographs she had already seen so many

times they were burned into her brain. Emma smiling back over a bare shoulder. A black dress. A tanned arm. Georgina knew the comments (*Gorgeous, hon!! Is it just me or do you keep getting younger??* and *Wifey material xx*), mostly from female friends, by heart.

Georgina wished *she* had a female friend to talk to. But she'd let her social life slide. There was no one she could call late at night. No one who would be reliably there at the other end of the phone, like women on TV always seemed to have. Like bloody *Sex and the City*. She had been preoccupied, with her life and her husband and her child, and she'd left so many messages unanswered it became too late to send one of her own.

In lieu of a friend, she turned to the internet. In bed in the dark, with the lights of passing cars throwing shadows on the ceiling, she used her phone to search the words *husband had a one-night stand*.

Many people had shared similar stories. Countless articles, blog posts and think pieces offered conflicting advice. On a public forum, Georgina read a comment that made her stomach turn over.

> Are you sure it was just a one-off? Cheaters only ever
> admit to a toned-down version of what they did. That
> way they can alleviate their guilt and get forgiveness
> while keeping their relationship. It's called trickle truth.

She opened another tab and searched: *trickle truth*.

> Trickle truth: When a cheater confesses to their partner
> but only admits minor details. More details may come

out as time goes on, but they will never give you the
full story. They confess just enough to remove their
own guilt.

That was what Bren had done in the beginning. And it had
worked. Georgina remembered her logic at the time. Surely
he was being honest, she had thought; after all, he'd chosen
to confess, of his own volition.

She'd been so naïve.

A user who called herself SusansMama wrote:

God, I wish I'd left when I first learnt about the affair.
Instead of hanging around for two years of 'working on
it', i.e. being gaslighted, cheated on and driven insane.
Before you make any decisions, MAKE SURE YOU
KNOW THE TRUTH.

Cleverusername replied:

'Make sure you know the truth' impossible. Cheaters
only let you see the tip of the iceberg.

The occasional comment offered a different perspective.
One woman, who called herself AnonymousForThis, wrote:

I cheated on my husband when I was twenty-five. A
one-night stand. It meant nothing. I never told him.
When you are young, such betrayals mean everything.
After four kids and twenty years, you know other things
are more important. But why hurt him by bringing it up
now? We have a good marriage. Solid. Every marriage

has its secrets. Sometimes I wonder what there is on *his* side that *I* don't know.

But most were full of dire warnings. Georgina lay in bed, phone above her face, features illuminated by greenish light, and read story after story of others who had been systematically fooled, manipulated, lied to.

Feeling sick, she added the words *ex-girlfriend* to her search:

ZaraT: Being unfaithful with an ex is worse. What if he's secretly been in love with her all along?

Georgina put her phone aside. She believed that you should never google your symptoms if you were feeling unwell; that reading a list of all the horrific diseases from which you might be dying would only trigger an unhelpful bout of hypochondria. Perhaps the same logic should be applied to infidelity. Her mind had already been alive with questions that agonised her. What had it been like between them in that hotel room? What positions did they do? Did Emma look better naked than she did? Did they hold each other after? Whisper in the dark, all guilty and intimate?

Now she felt even worse.

Was there more that Bren wasn't telling her? How could she ever know?

16

In the immediate aftermath of Bren's revelation, Georgina tried to maintain her distance. She could not drop everything and rush off dramatically to stay in a hotel like a character in a movie. There was Cody to think about; there was reality. But she asked Bren to back off, to let her breathe, to save his endless apologies and self-admonishments until she was ready to hear them, and to her relief, he complied.

That was why, on Friday, she found herself out walking at dusk, having taken the observation 'We're out of milk' as an excuse to get out of the house.

She took the long route home from the shops. Late afternoon was fading into a cloudless, frost-crusted evening. Past the trees and red-brick houses, past the bookies and pubs, Georgina walked and thought, wrapped up warm against the biting cold.

Trickle truth.

Alleviate their guilt.

Never give the full story.

How did anyone handle this not knowing? It was killing her. If there was footage of the night Bren and Emma had spent together, she would watch every second of it. An unhealthy thing to wish for, perhaps, but at least then she'd know what it was she was being asked to forgive.

The main road was busy, with cars passing and a rowdy group of students drinking at the bus stop. A sudden scream caused Georgina to spin around. The person screamed again, and she realised it was just one of the drunken students. Jumpy, she chided herself.

She turned off the main road. Past the derelict house on the corner, its boarded-up windows scrawled with spray-paint slogans (*Irish women won't wait – repeal the 8th!*), and onto a quieter, less well-lit street. As the bustle of the main road faded behind her, Georgina could hear the *swish-swish* sound the shopping bag made as it brushed against her jeans.

It had reached that precise moment when evening trembles between dusk and night. The sky was a purple so deep it was almost black. A few faint tendrils of ghost-grey cloud trailed across the rising moon.

Georgina walked briskly along. *Swish-swish* went the bag. *Click-clack* went her low heels on the concrete, the sound echoing out—

Was that an echo, or someone else's footsteps?

Georgina glanced over her shoulder. There was nobody in sight.

She began to walk a little faster. *Swish-swish*. *Click-clack*. And—

There it was again. Footsteps.

This time she turned sharply. And saw something. Movement.

About thirty feet back, where the shadows were thick, she could have sworn she saw someone duck behind a tree.

She stood still, her heart pounding.

Why don't you walk back and see for yourself? she thought.

And then: don't be silly, there's nobody there.

And on the heels of that thought came the clearest, the one that made her gut clench: There *is* somebody there, and that's exactly why you should go straight home, right now.

Georgina took one slow step backwards. Then another.

Turning, she began to walk in the direction of her house as fast as she could without breaking into a jog. Looking back over her shoulder she saw the unmistakable shape of a person stepping out from behind the tree.

She ran the final stretch, grocery bag swinging madly. She could see her house – she was nearly there – that familiar wooden door behind which lay warmth, safety . . .

She ran up the short driveway, fumbling in her pocket for her keys, got the door open, half fell inside, and slammed it shut. In the hallway she stood, heart pounding.

'Georgina? Is that you?' Bren called down the stairs.

'It's me.' She dropped the grocery bag and put her eye to the peephole of the door. The street seemed deserted.

Being inside her own home, hearing Bren upstairs took the edge off the fear she had felt. *Fear* – was that the aim? If somebody out there was trying to scare her, they had succeeded.

But she was already less afraid.

She opened the front door again. Cold flooded the warm hallway.

'Georgina? You going back out?'

Forty-eight hours ago, she would have asked Bren to come with her. Even if he'd raised his eyebrows sceptically at her story of being followed, even if she'd suspected he was only humouring her, it would have been a relief to have him by her side. But that was forty-eight hours ago. Now . . .

'I think I dropped something,' she replied. 'Just going out to check.'

She took out her smartphone, turned on the torch and strode back outside. She looked up towards that darker stretch of street, where the person had stepped out from behind the tree. She couldn't see anyone now.

I'm not afraid, Georgina told herself, and began to walk.

She'd never noticed before just how dark this upper stretch of road was at night. Several of the streetlights were in need of replacement. Someone should write a strongly worded letter to Dublin city council about it.

I'm not afraid.

As she walked, Georgina kept her gaze focused on the tree the person had hidden behind. The light from her phone illuminated the spaces between trees and behind wheelie bins, places she had never previously thought of as corners in which someone could hide.

I'm not afraid.

But her mouth was dry as she shone the light behind the tree.

Nothing but concrete. If someone *had* been here, they were gone.

'Georgina,' said a voice behind her.

She screamed.

Clutching her phone like a weapon, she spun around to see Anthony. He was standing about a foot away, a very confused expression on his face.

'I didn't mean to scare you.' He was wearing a hat and scarf, and appeared to be out for a stroll. 'Are you all right?'

'I'm fine.' She tried to steady her breathing. 'Sorry. You just ... startled me.'

'Looking for something?'

'What? No.' Her heart was beating wildly. 'I mean yes. My earring. I dropped it.'

Anthony frowned. 'You sure you're all right, Georgina?' he said, more seriously this time.

'Me? I'm grand.' Georgina half laughed, a nervous habit she fell back on sometimes, and groped around mentally for a change of subject. 'What about yourself, Anthony? Hey, last weekend, did we see you out digging in your garden at night?' Striving for light and jovial, she remembered the joke Bren had made at the time and repeated it: 'Burying a body, were you?'

Anthony didn't laugh. In the heartbeat of silence that followed, she knew she had said something wrong.

'Dunno what you're talking about,' he said gruffly.

Georgina stared at him.

Anthony made an aggressive shrugging motion. 'I've got a bus to catch, Georgina. See you later.' And he strode off.

She watched him go. What on earth ...

That was a lie. He'd lied right to her face. But why?

17

Bren was waiting for her in the hall. 'Everything all right?'

Georgina looked into the front room for a reassuring glimpse of Cody on the sofa, watching *Zootopia* for the twentieth time. She breathed in the sight of him there, safe.

'Did you find it?' Bren asked in the self-consciously attentive tone with which he'd been addressing her since she'd learnt he had sex with Emma.

'Find what?'

Bren looked puzzled. 'Whatever it was that you dropped.'

Georgina blinked, her brain taking several seconds to catch up. 'Oh. Yeah. I found it.'

Why had Anthony lied?

'Come into the kitchen,' she said. 'I need to talk to you.'

He followed her, his face all hangdog and sorry, obviously expecting the topic to be the state of their marriage.

'Something strange just happened. On my way home.' Georgina closed the kitchen door so Cody wouldn't overhear.

There seemed little point in telling sceptical Bren about figures behind trees, so she skipped ahead to 'I ran into Anthony, and he said the weirdest thing.'

She recapped the exchange. When she finished, Bren gave a long exhale.

'Yeah,' he said eventually, still in that carefully contrite voice. 'That's a bit strange all right.'

There was something unspoken in the silence that followed.

'He lied about it,' Georgina reiterated. 'He outright lied. Then he got all cagey and defensive and ran off. What do you think it means?'

'I don't know, Georgina.' Bren sounded a little more like his normal self as he went on: 'Anthony's a weird bloke. Grumpy old bastard, too. I've been saying it for years, but you always defend him.'

'I always thought he was a softie underneath,' she said. 'The way he talks about his granddaughter . . .'

She trailed off. Something had occurred to her. Something she'd never realised before.

'Have you ever actually seen Lily?' she asked Bren.

'Who?'

'Lily, Anthony's granddaughter!' she said impatiently. 'The one he talks about *all* the time. I've never seen her. She never comes to visit him at the house. Come to think of it, have you ever seen *any* visitor at Anthony's house?'

'I guess I haven't,' said Bren slowly.

'That's weird, isn't it?' Georgina's skin was prickling.

Then she saw Bren's expression.

'Oh, come on!' she said. 'You've got to admit that it's odd.'

Bren removed his glasses and pinched the bridge of his nose.

'Being eccentric isn't a crime, Georgie,' he said. 'Neither is being lonely.'

'I never said ...' She felt wrong-footed. 'I just want to know what he's lying about.'

'If you wanted me to make a legitimate guess? I'd say anyone burying stuff out their back garden at night is holding drugs for someone. Or dodgy cash.'

'Come on, Bren, at his age?'

'Okay then.' Bren put his glasses back on and looked at her. 'Maybe Anthony was gardening in the dark. Maybe he's barking mad. I don't know what the neighbours are doing with their lives, Georgina, but I do know this: it has nothing to do with Cody's imaginary game. *Nothing.*'

So he did know what she was thinking.

Abandoning all pretence, she said: 'How can you *know* that, though?'

'I just do. How can you possibly think ...' He broke off. When he spoke again, his voice was more controlled. 'Look, Georgie. I know you've been having a ... difficult time.'

She couldn't help but laugh coldly. 'And whose fault is that?'

He looked miserable. 'I know I've added to it, and I'm sorry. I'm sorry I lied about what me and Emma ...'

Her stomach turned over. '*Don't.*'

'... about what we did that night,' he persisted, 'and I'm sorrier than you'll ever know that any of it happened in the first place. I fucked up. But I love you, Georgie, and right now, I'm worried about you.' He took a deep breath. 'This is going to sound patronising, but I have to say it. You're not thinking straight. You're grieving, you're stressed, you're sleep-deprived ...'

'So?' She was struggling to keep up. She wished he hadn't said Emma's name.

'So,' Bren said, 'maybe Anthony didn't lie.'

Georgina blinked, thrown.

'Maybe you didn't see what you thought you saw. It was dark, you only saw him for a second . . .'

What? '*No.* I saw him. Behind the shed, digging.'

'How could you see him if he was behind the shed?'

'Because of the *angle*,' she said indignantly. 'Go up to the bathroom and look for yourself. We can see behind Anthony's shed – not the ground, but if there's someone standing—'

'Georgina,' he cut across her, 'you haven't slept properly in weeks. Do you *know* what lack of sleep does to the human brain?'

Georgina was silent, and Bren continued in earnest psychology-graduate mode. 'Sleep deprivation is serious. It impairs mental function. It can cause hallucinations.'

She shook her head. 'I saw Anthony digging in his garden in the middle of the night, I know I did, and he lied about it.'

'Georgie,' said Bren, in his gentlest voice, 'you know yourself how the mind can play tricks. I mean, you've had problems before with—'

She flinched. 'This is *nothing* like that!'

The shadows. The clock. The stuffed toy.

How could Bren use that against her now?

'I'm not saying it's the same. All I'm saying is, why not go to Better Steps and have a chat with . . . Georgina. Wait!'

But she was walking out of the room. She closed the door hard behind her.

Hallucinations . . .

Maybe you didn't see what you thought you saw . . .

No, Georgina thought fiercely.

She knew what she had seen.

Didn't she?

18

The following morning, Georgina slipped into Cody's bedroom while he and Bren were downstairs having breakfast. From there she peered into Anthony's garden, hoping for a glimpse of the freshly dug earth that would prove Anthony had been lying. But the ground behind the shed wasn't visible. Just as from the bathroom window, while she'd be able to see someone standing there, she couldn't see the soil.

Craning her neck made no difference. Neither did standing on tiptoe or pressing her face against the window. All she achieved was the circle of fog her breath made on the glass.

Maybe you didn't see what you thought you saw . . .

'Mam!' Cody's footsteps sounded on the stairs. 'Are you awake? Do you know where my shoes are?'

Georgina hurried out onto the landing. Cody was standing there.

'What were you doing in my room?'

'Looking for your shoes, silly,' Georgina said smoothly. 'Let's check downstairs, shall we?'

Bren had spent the past two nights on the sofa in the front room, waking early to ensure his makeshift bed was tidied away before Cody could see it. When they went downstairs, both front room and kitchen were spotless. 'I made you breakfast,' Bren announced. A plate of scrambled eggs sat obsequiously on the table. The sight made Georgina feel a sudden, huge rage, coupled with the urge to do something completely unlike herself, like fling the plate of eggs across the room. Why not? Other people smashed things when their spouses were unfaithful. She saw it on TV.

'I'm not hungry,' she said.

Cody ate the scrambled eggs. It was Saturday, and Bren was bringing him to the Phoenix Park. Georgina had work. She grabbed a banana before she left, kissed Cody on the head and said goodbye to Bren without looking at him.

The bookshop was quiet that day, leaving Georgina to occupy time with her fragmented thoughts. Her brain kept replaying the moment Bren had said 'me and Emma'. That had hurt. Hearing their names linked together like that.

'Excuse me,' asked a customer politely, 'do you have any good mysteries?'

Georgina led him to the right section, her mind far off, obsessing over her own mystery. Anthony digging behind his shed in the dark. His gruff denial: *Dunno what you're talking about.*

Why was he lying?

She drove home in a state of distraction, car horns blaring as she failed to notice a light turn green. When she arrived at the house, it was empty. Dark and quiet. She checked her phone. A message informed her that Bren and Cody had gone to Tesco. They'd just left.

Georgina walked out to the back garden. It was another cold, clear night. Her breath turned to mist on the air. There was a single star visible in the evening sky.

At Vera's, all the lights were on. The muffled sound of some radio talk-show floated from the kitchen.

There were no lights on in Anthony's house.

She drifted across to the wall that separated her garden from Anthony's, moving casually in case somebody was watching. Not that she thought anyone was, but just in case. She shot a furtive glance up at Anthony's house, trying to shake the feeling that those windows were watchful eyes. They were glass, just glass.

When she reached the wall, Georgina leant against it – trying, and failing, to look nonchalant – and peered over at the earth behind Anthony's shed.

However, the area by the shed was where Anthony kept his wheelie bins. They blocked her view of the ground.

Abandoning her casual act completely, she stepped up on a flowerpot and stuck her head over the wall.

But those damn wheelie bins! They completely obscured her view.

Georgina thought about what she was going to do for only a second before she did it. Any further consideration would have caused her to lose her nerve.

She swung a leg up, vaulted over the wall and landed with a thud in Anthony's garden.

As her feet hit the concrete, Georgina could barely believe what she was doing. But thudding in her ears, along with her heartbeat, was a pulse of determination.

Deluded, was she? Imagining things?

With footsteps soft as cats' paws, she crept around the bins, throwing a frightened glance at Anthony's back door.

Imagine Bren could see this, some wry part of her mind observed. *You really do look like you've lost the plot now.* She fought a ludicrous urge to burst into nervous giggles.

Then she stepped around the bins and looked down at the ground, and the desire to laugh completely died.

Behind the shed was a small, square patch of freshly turned earth.

Georgina stared down at it. Images raced through her mind. Stick-figure drawings. Golden wrappers. Broken pots.

Buried right there was the final puzzle piece. She was sure of it.

For a moment, the urge to sneak into Anthony's shed, grab a shovel and start digging was so strong she had to struggle to contain it.

That really *would* be crazy.

Her heart was racing. She was so close.

Don't be insane. Go back. Now.

Her sensible side won. Quietly she crept from behind the shed and towards the wall.

At that moment, a light came on in Anthony's kitchen, illuminating the garden.

Georgina ducked back behind the shed, blood thumping wildly.

Had he seen her?

Motionless in the dark, she counted slowly to ten. Nothing further happened. She counted to ten again. Still Anthony didn't come outside. She must be safe.

But how was she going to get through that patch of light and into her own garden without being seen?

Just as she was considering this dilemma, she heard Anthony's back door open with a slight squeak.

Her heart stopped. Or at least that was how it felt; it seemed to actually falter and pause in her chest before thudding against her breastbone with extra strength on the next beat.

She heard Anthony's footsteps cross the concrete.

He knows you're here.

He was just feet away from her. He was moving around the shed.

She had seconds left. She could try to scramble over the wall into the next garden and call for help . . .

But instead she stood there, immobile, as if she were watching her life from the outside.

It wasn't just that she was paralysed with fear. She needed to know what would happen next. She needed answers.

Anthony stepped around the corner. He was gripping a shovel with both hands like a baseball bat. How had she never noticed before just how stocky Anthony was, how powerfully built?

And now he was standing in front of her, holding a shovel, and there was nowhere to run.

19

'*Georgina?*'

Anthony took a step forward and Georgina cringed back against the wall. He followed her frightened gaze to the shovel in his hands and lowered it apologetically.

'I thought you were a burglar.' He was wearing old grey tracksuit bottoms, a creased T-shirt, no shoes, and an expression of utter confusion. 'Jaysis, Georgina, what're you doing?'

He was now holding the shovel rather awkwardly, as if unsure what to do with it. He moved it to his left hand and stretched out his right to Georgina, who was still cowering against the wall.

But Georgina didn't take it. She wouldn't be lulled into a false sense of security. *Anthony had lied.*

She straightened up by herself.

Anthony withdrew his hand, looking more baffled than ever.

'Are you all right, Georgina?' he asked, very gently. 'Do you need help?'

He had no idea what she was doing, she realised. His gaze did not flicker guiltily to the patch of dug-up earth. Whatever was buried there, whatever he'd lied about, it was nothing to do with her and Cody.

On the heels of that realisation, several questions hit her like punches.

What *was* she doing? Why had she climbed into Anthony's garden? Was Bren right? Was she losing her mind?

'I don't know what I'm doing,' she said weakly. 'I don't . . .'

She trailed off. Anthony stared at her, obviously at a bit of a loss. Then he made a sort of helpless gesture with the hand that wasn't holding the shovel and said, 'Should we keep standing here like a pair of eejits, or d'you want to come inside for a cup of tea?'

Minutes later, she found herself at Anthony's kitchen table while the kettle boiled.

'D'you take sugar, Georgina?' asked Anthony, busying himself with tea bags. He had stepped into a pair of tartan slippers.

'No thanks,' said Georgina, slightly dazed. If someone had told her half an hour ago that she would end up sitting here . . .

Anthony's home was the tidy, self-contained space of a person living alone. There was one of everything: one neat place set at the table, one mug and saucer drying by the sink. Standing against the wall was an empty rabbit hutch.

Anthony put a cup of milky tea down in front of her.

Georgina, who had accepted the offer only to lend this encounter some semblance of normality, thanked him and pretended to sip it.

He sat down across from her. 'D'you want to tell me what's going on, Georgina?'

There was such kindness in his voice that a lump rose in Georgina's throat.

'Can I ask you something first?' she said, relieved her voice didn't crack.

'Go on.'

'Why did you lie to me about being out in the garden the other night?'

Anthony looked sheepish.

'Is that what all this is about?' He rubbed his face and sighed. 'It's stupid, Georgina. I was embarrassed. It's ...' He paused. 'Remember I was telling you about the rabbit I bought for my granddaughter?'

'The one that ended up living with you.' Georgina remembered. *What has the rabbit got to do with any of this?*

'Well, I kind of got used to her,' Anthony went on. 'I didn't realise rabbits had so much personality. She'd follow me around the house, and when she wanted attention, she'd stamp her back legs, like this ...' He made a *thump-thump-thump* with his hand against the table. 'I always thought rabbits were stupid, but Cupcake—'

'Cupcake?' Georgina repeated before she could stop herself.

'Well, Lily picked the name, didn't she? I wasn't planning on keeping her. I thought I'd bring her back to the pet shop, but then I started thinking. What if she ended up with some kid who didn't look after her, forgot to feed her? I couldn't let that happen. So Cupcake stayed here with me. She'd sit on my lap when I was watching telly, like a cat. I didn't know rabbits did that.'

He looked sadly at the empty hutch, and Georgina could see where this story was going.

'Maybe I should've called a vet. She seemed a bit quiet that day, but I didn't think much of it. I went to the pub, and when I got back, she was lying dead on the straw. I felt terrible. Dunno what I did wrong. I didn't want to leave her lying there, so I brought her out the back and buried her. I'd had a few drinks, like I said, and it just seemed like the decent thing to do.'

He gave the empty hutch another sad glance. 'I'll have to make a story up for Lily next time I see her. Cupcake went to live on a farm, or something.'

Georgina's mind had gone blank. His *rabbit*. When Bren heard about this . . .

But of course she couldn't tell Bren any of this.

'So,' said Anthony. He was watching her intently. 'Now. D'you want to tell me what you were doing in my garden?'

Georgina looked down at the table. 'I know it sounds mental, but I needed to know what you were burying.'

'I'm not going to lie, Georgina,' said Anthony, kindly but bluntly, 'that does sound pretty mental. Been watching too many crime shows, have you?'

He was watching her closely, but Georgina couldn't bring herself to meet his eyes. She stared instead at the faded tattoos on his arms, blurred lines of ink bleeding together. 'Anthony, I'm sorry. I've been under a lot of stress . . .'

How to explain Cody's game? Or Bren and Emma?

She settled for: 'I've been having personal problems. And I think – I think some of it might be happening inside my head. Some of it is very much in the real world, but . . .' She broke off and kneaded her temple with her fingertips. 'My husband thinks I should go and talk to someone.'

Anthony nodded. 'A head doctor? That could be a good idea.' But his pale blue eyes were shrewd. 'What, d'you not want to?'

'Well . . .' Georgina hesitated. 'Going to a doctor means admitting something's wrong, doesn't it? I've had episodes in the past where my mental health got bad. Like, very bad. I don't want to go back there. I don't want to admit it might be happening again.'

The words came out in a rush. She hadn't admitted that to herself yet, let alone anyone else. She felt embarrassed then, but Anthony's face was kind and listening.

'In my day,' he said, 'if you lost your marbles or you just couldn't manage, you'd go talk to a priest. I still go to confession sometimes, myself. I always feel better after. Sort of . . . clearer, after getting everything off my chest. I can't imagine my life without that.' Anthony's expression was earnest. 'I know it's not what young people do nowadays, going to priests. And I know the Church has done some terrible things in this country, but maybe talking to a doctor helps in the same sort of way. The best thing to do if you need help, love, is just to ask for it.'

They sat for a while in companionable silence, Anthony, with his tattooed arms and his tartan slippers, drinking his tea like this was a perfectly normal social situation.

Presently Georgina said: 'Can I ask you something else, Anthony?'

He nodded.

'Your granddaughter, Lily? Could I see a photo of her?'

Anthony's blue eyes brightened. He passed her his phone, open on a photo of a beautiful child with a massive grin and hair bunched into two pigtails.

'That's our Lily,' he said. 'Isn't she gorgeous?'

Georgina nodded. 'Yeah, she is.'

She knew her next question was a loaded one, and she asked it tentatively.

'Does she ever visit you here?'

Anthony was silent for a moment. He took the phone back and put it in his pocket. He exhaled heavily. 'My son and I . . .' He stopped.

'You don't have to tell me if you don't want to,' Georgina hastened to say.

'No, it's all right,' he said. 'You were honest with me, I'll be honest with you. I wasn't the greatest husband. Always on the drink in those days. Did terrible selfish things.' He kept his gaze on the table as he spoke. 'I'd an awful temper back then. I never hit her – never – but I frightened her, and I frightened the kid. In the end, they left. It took me years to sort myself out, and by the time I did, my son was nearly grown. He's never really forgiven me for being what I was when he was small.'

Anthony looked up now.

'And I don't blame him, I don't. I'm just glad he's giving me a chance to be part of Lily's life. D'you know, this Christmas just gone was the first I've spent with my family in a long time. Watching Lily open her presents on Christmas morning . . .' His face split into a huge smile. 'Jaysis, it makes a difference having people, doesn't it?'

Georgina nodded. Her throat was tight.

'My son says,' Anthony continued, and here he sat up a

little straighter, 'that I can take Lily on a day out soon. To the cinema, or a funfair. Just the two of us, y'know.'

The pride on his face made Georgina want to cry.

'I want her to remember me as the grandad who brought her places, and bought her presents, and always remembered her birthday. That's the only goal in my life now.'

When she trusted herself to speak, Georgina said, 'That's lovely, Anthony. She'll have those memories forever. I didn't mean to pry ...'

'No, not at all. Good to talk about it, actually.'

There was a moment of somewhat heavy silence, which Anthony broke with a grin.

'D'you know,' he said, 'it's good to get to know your neighbours like this, isn't it? People should break into each other's gardens more often.'

Georgina stared at him for a single heartbeat, and then they both began to laugh. The inappropriateness of it only made her laugh harder.

'It's really ... not ... funny,' she managed between gasps. 'I should be apologising, not laughing.'

'Ah Georgina,' said Anthony, wiping his eyes, 'I promise I won't hold it against you.'

When the waves of laughter finally subsided, Georgina took her phone out of her pocket and checked the time.

'God, Anthony, I better go,' she said, getting to her feet. 'Bren'll be home any minute.'

'Ah,' said Anthony. 'And you don't want him to know you've been climbing into the neighbours' gardens, is that it?'

'Honestly, no. I'd rather not tell him just yet.' She wanted space to wrap her own head around what was happening first. 'You won't mention it to him, will you?'

Anthony stood up. 'I won't,' he assured her as he walked her to the door, 'as long as you promise me one thing. I want you to promise to look after yourself, you hear?'

Georgina had to fight the urge to hug Anthony right there in his doorway.

'I'll try,' she said.

20

Later that night, Georgina took a long, long shower. To get away from Bren. To be alone under the hot water and let her thoughts swirl.

The stick-figure drawings. The golden wrappers.

Cody's voice: *I made her up.*

And Bren's: *I'm worried about you, Georgina.*

She twisted the shower handle, turning the heat up. One thing Bren was right about. She *had* had problems like this before.

The shadows. The clock. The stuffed toy.

Tilting her face up to the water, Georgina forced herself to remember.

It was right after Cody was born. Her pregnancy had been healthy, and the birth not particularly difficult. Her hospital bed had been surrounded by friends, family and flowers.

She'd been totally unprepared for what happened next. She hadn't even known it was something that *could* happen. She'd heard of the baby blues, of course – sadness, tiredness, disillusionment – and braced herself for a spell of those. But nobody had told her there was a possibility of something more serious.

Had it already been starting in the hospital? Georgina didn't know.

All she knew for sure was that she first noticed it when they brought Cody home. She and Bren arrived back at their old house in Phibsboro, laden with toys and flowers and a new son, and that night, it began in earnest.

Every time she closed her eyes, Georgina saw graphic, horrifying images. Sometimes Cody was being smothered by a faceless man. Other times she just saw her baby dead, his tiny face blue and lifeless.

On their third night home, Georgina woke screaming from a dream where the person holding the pillow over Cody's face was her.

After assuring Bren it was just a nightmare, the details of which she couldn't remember, she tiptoed into Cody's room to make sure he was still alive. Of course he was, days old and beautiful, fast asleep under his blue blanket.

That was when the voice first spoke to her. Loud and clear. It was a man's voice, right there in the room with her, and it said: 'You're going to smother your baby. And if you don't, I will.'

Georgina knew several things at that point. She knew the voice she could hear belonged to the faceless man from her nightmares. She knew the faceless man was currently hiding in one of Cody's stuffed toys, a blue elephant with floppy ears and the words *It's a boy!* sewn into its tummy.

She also knew that all of this sounded completely crazy. She feared that if she told anyone what was happening, nobody would believe her, and they might try to take her baby away from her.

In the days after the voice first spoke to her, the delusions accelerated rapidly. Georgina became convinced she could make things happen with her mind – but only terrible things. She began to believe that if she looked at the clock in the kitchen while it was striking the hour, Cody would stop breathing.

Georgina lived in terror of looking at that clock at the wrong moment. But even if she managed not to, Cody still wasn't safe. The faceless man lurked in the shadows. He moved in the periphery of her vision, but when she looked at him directly, he melted back into the walls. She knew he was waiting for his chance to harm her son.

She threw every pillow in the house out into the garden and wouldn't tell Bren why. She hid the stuffed elephant in a box under the stairs. She covered her eyes when she crossed the kitchen to avoid looking at the clock. But despite all her precautions, she still woke screaming at night from dreams where she held a pillow over Cody's face until his little legs stopped kicking.

Thank God for Bren. He recognised her symptoms and took her to a psychiatrist. He made sure she took her meds. He helped her understand what was happening to her.

'Think of post-partum psychosis as your brain reacting to this huge shift in your life,' he said. 'All your fears come back to wanting to protect Cody. Because you're a good mother. A parent's anxieties keep their child alive. Your brain just got a bit carried away.'

Bren made her feel like it had come from a good place, like maybe she wasn't a terrible mother after all.

She took her meds, saw her psychiatrist and started therapy. They bought new pillows and threw the stuffed elephant away. The shadows stopped moving. Things got better — though it was a long time before Georgina could look at the kitchen clock again.

The heat and steam of the shower was suddenly dizzying. Georgina turned the water off, got out and grabbed a towel.

No matter how angry she was with Bren, no matter how raw her hurt, he'd been by her side through so much. She didn't know how she would have coped without him back then.

Still, Georgina struggled to accept his help this time. Right now, their marriage was on the line because of him. And he was telling *her* to see a therapist? She wasn't the one who'd jumped into bed with an ex.

Then again, she conceded as she towelled herself dry, she was the one who'd just been caught trespassing in a neighbour's garden.

Maybe Bren had a point.

Perhaps she should give it a try, she thought as she got dressed. Talk to a professional. Open her mind to the possibility that her mental health was playing some role in whatever was going on. It couldn't hurt, could it?

But something inside her thought that it *could* hurt somehow. A part of her was still screaming, *Something is very wrong! Grab Cody and run! Get out of this house!*

Georgina stared at herself in the bathroom mirror. That voice sounded like her mothering instincts. But as she well knew, instincts could go haywire.

Maybe Cody wasn't in any danger — at least no more than anyone else moving through this perilous world. Perhaps it *was* all in her head.

21

Before bed the following evening, Georgina told Bren she was open to seeking professional help.

'That's brilliant, Georgina.' He was enthusiastic. 'Great news. I'll call Better Steps first thing tomorrow.'

She got under the duvet and rolled onto her side.

'I know I've been the world's shittiest husband,' Bren continued, 'but I love you, Georgie. I just want to see you happy again.'

She said, 'Will you turn off the lights?'

With a sigh, he did so. She felt him settle on the far side of the mattress. They'd decided that Bren should come back to their shared bed so Cody wouldn't catch him on the sofa, but they slept with a foot of space between them.

After a minute's silence, Bren said, 'You know, if you ever want to try couple's counselling, I'd be up for that.'

Jesus. 'One thing at a time,' Georgina said.

'Right. Course,' said Bren's voice in the dark. 'Well, goodnight.'

Georgina lay wide awake, wondering what her new therapist would be like. Would they want to discuss her recent bereavement? Some part of her railed against the idea of talking about her mother to a stranger. How could someone who hadn't even *known* Rose understand her loss?

She wanted her mother. The want was simple and earth-shattering and unrelenting. There was a little girl inside her, stamping her foot, shouting at the stars. *I want my mother.*

She shifted in the bed, tried to get comfortable, adjusting her pillow. She wondered what her mother would have had to say about mysterious lollipops, broken pots and feelings of being watched. Rose might have suspected something supernatural was afoot. She had believed firmly in the afterlife, in angels, and that a sighting of a robin was a sign a loved one was watching over you.

Georgina remembered the person who'd followed her down the street, the sound of their footsteps, the sight of them ducking behind the tree. She could've *sworn* there was someone there . . .

Then again, post-partum, she could've sworn there was a faceless man living in her walls.

Restless, she rolled onto her back. She had never shared her mother's beliefs, but right now, she envied them. To believe in anything other than cold, hard facts would be a relief. The idea that she couldn't trust her own mind frightened her more than any ghost.

The following afternoon, she popped in to visit her dad on the way home from work. Jimmy seemed in good humour, but Georgina didn't trust it. If anyone needed to discuss their bereavement with a professional, it was her father. But Irish men of his generation, his background, didn't search their feelings. Jimmy would make no attempt to reimagine his old age. However many years he had left, he would simply spend them waiting to join Rose.

'How's Cody?' he asked as he led her into the kitchen. But Georgina didn't answer. She was distracted. Her father was chewing something, and as he put the wrapper in the bin, the glint of gold caught her attention.

'What's that, Dad?'

'D'you want one?' And he reached into the cupboard and took out a glass jar of toffees.

Georgina took one, but not to eat. She read the words stamped across the wrapper. CAFFREY'S CONFECTIONERY.

'Do you usually buy these toffees, Dad?'

'When I can get them. There's a shop in town that sells them, and I always buy some when I'm in. Best toffees in Ireland.'

'And I suppose,' said Georgina, realisation dawning, 'that you give them to Cody sometimes.'

'Oh, Cody loves them,' said Jimmy. He unwrapped another. 'They're terrible for your teeth, of course, but I can't resist. You can't beat the old sweets.'

Georgina stared down at the gold-wrapped sweet in her hand. So this was where Cody had got the toffees. Nothing sinister. Just Jimmy spoiling his grandson again. Georgina could picture Cody hiding the handfuls of sweets his grand-father slipped him, just like he slipped him twenty-euro notes ('Don't tell your mother . . . .'). She could picture the toffee wrapper falling from Cody's pocket as he played in the bushes, and being picked up the next day by her own hand. Her paranoid mind had seen patterns where there were none.

'My friend Seamus down the road lost a tooth in a toffee,' Jimmy said musingly, 'so perhaps at my age, they're best avoided.'

He looked at the chewy sweet, shrugged and popped it into his mouth.

That evening, when Georgina turned onto her own street, everything seemed quiet. The lights were on in Anthony's house. The smell of fresh baking drifted from Vera's.

She unlocked her front door and stepped into the hall. Cody was playing in the front room, sprawled on the patch-work rug in front of the fireplace. He was surrounded by an assortment of teddy bears, Transformers and toy soldiers.

'Hi, Mam,' he said, carefully organising his soldiers into a neat line. 'Do you want to be in my game?'

Georgina's heart swelled with love for him.

'In a minute, sweetie,' she said, taking off her coat.

'You can be the green teddy.' Cody was lining up more toys. 'This one is Grandad . . . This is Old Granny . . . And this one is New Granny!'

Georgina's stomach clenched.

Cody, cheerfully oblivious, continued, 'And this is a dragon, and this is his friend who's a monster . . .'

Dragons and monsters. Imaginary friends, imaginary games. It sounded so benign and banal, all tossed together like that. The natural products of a child's imagination.

Bren, who had walked into the hall just in time to over-hear, was looking at her with concern.

'I'm fine,' she said to him quietly. 'Really, I'm fine. What's up?'

'Good news,' said Bren. He took her coat and hung it up

for her. 'I called Better Steps and got you an appointment for Saturday at two. We're lucky they were able to take you at such short notice. They had a cancellation.'

'Thank you.' Georgina knew she should feel grateful, but what she felt was cornered.

'I'm proud of you, Georgie,' Bren said earnestly. 'Really. I know it can be hard to ask for help.'

He reached for her, but she stepped away. His hands fell back down by his sides.

'Mam! Come be in the game!'

Georgina broke away from Bren's wounded gaze and went to join Cody on the rug.

'So I'm the green teddy, am I? Tell me what to do.'

Cody made his dragon breathe fire down on the army of toys. Bren was watching from the door. For Cody's sake, Georgina gave him a fake smile.

'Mam, pay attention,' said Cody sternly. 'The dragon is coming for you next. If you're not careful, you'll get all burnt up.'

22

The next day, Bren was off work early and collected Cody from after-school, allowing Georgina the rare treat of being able to leave work at her own pace. Remembering Anthony's advice – *Promise to look after yourself* – Georgina took the time to pop into the café next to the bookshop and buy herself a hot drink and a slice of lemon cake. She ate slowly, enjoying the warm, bustling atmosphere of the busy little café.

On Saturday she had her first appointment with the Better Steps therapist who she hoped would help her begin the process of controlling her anxious thoughts. That was looking after herself, wasn't it? Anthony would be pleased.

She finished her tea and cake at a leisurely pace, then headed home. She kept a sharp eye on the road as she let herself into the house. But all she saw was a young man with a guitar case leaving the house of the students who sometimes threw noisy parties. A scruffy-looking cat running across the street. The Brazilian couple from number 24 walking by with arms linked and heads close together, entirely focused on each other.

Nothing seemed out of the ordinary at all.

Once she was in the door, Cody rushed at her, a ball of limbs and energy. 'Mam!'

'Hello, sweetie.' Georgina crouched to embrace him. The smell of his skin, his little arms around her neck – sometimes it overwhelmed her. Hit her like a freight train. The love.

She remembered what Bren had said after her diagnosis of post-partum psychosis. *All your fears come back to wanting to protect Cody. Because you're a good mother.*

Later, when Cody was reading in bed, Bren approached her in the kitchen. 'How're you feeling, Georgie?'

'Okay.' Despite herself, all Georgina wanted was to ask if anything suspicious had happened that afternoon. Any phone calls, any strangers lingering on the road a little too long.

Bren seemed to know what was on her mind. He said, without any irony, 'I didn't notice anything strange all afternoon. Cody was fine. No mention of the granny game.'

She nodded.

He said hesitantly. 'I was wondering if we could talk . . . '

'Bren, please. I told you. I need space.' Whenever Bren wanted to talk about him and Emma, Georgina felt like she couldn't breathe.

With an almost comically wounded expression – which grated; *he* wasn't the one who'd been cheated on – off he went, leaving Georgina to drink her cup of chamomile tea in peace.

There should be someplace you could send a philandering spouse for a few weeks while you organised your thoughts. It didn't seem fair that he was right there, breathing down her neck, while she was still reeling from the shock. If they were rich, she could ship him off to a hotel. If they had a big house, they could disappear to opposite ends. But when you lived in a poky little north Dublin two-bedroom, there weren't a whole lot of options. Perhaps, Georgina thought, there was a business opportunity there. Disgraced partner camp? Get rid of your unfaithful husband or wife for a few weeks? But wait – she spotted the glaring flaw in her business model. All those cheaters shut up on top of one another? A recipe for disaster, surely.

'Georgie?' Bren interrupted her absurd train of thought. 'Cody wants you to tuck him in.'

'I'll be up in a minute.'

Upstairs, she found Cody with his nose in a book and his reading lamp on. Georgina smiled.

'Time for lights off, my love,' she said.

'One more chapter!'

'Did you brush your teeth already?'

'Yes!'

'Okay.' She sat down beside him. 'One more chapter. Do you want me to read it to you?'

'Yes.' Cody beamed at her. There was a small, dark smudge on his left cheek.

Georgina reached out a finger to brush it. 'What's that?'

'What?' Cody scrubbed at his face. Another trace of something dark stained the corner of his mouth.

'Cody.' She recognised the signs. 'You've been eating chocolate in bed again, haven't you?'

'No.' He was rubbing at his face frantically now, desperate to wipe away the evidence.

'Cody, no sweets after we brush our teeth, you know this. It defeats the whole purpose of brushing teeth.' She groped under his pillow, searching for the hidden goods. 'Where's the chocolate?'

'I ate it all.'

'*Really.*' Last time this happened, Georgina had found an entire tub of Nutella under Cody's pillow. 'Go on, you, go brush your teeth again.'

She pushed him gently off the bed. He stood on the carpet staring at her.

'*Go,*' she said, exasperated. 'Do you want your teeth to get all rotten?'

'The chocolate's gone,' Cody insisted. 'I ate it all.'

Georgina paused. Why did he seem so anxious? What didn't he want her to find? He stood watching, tense, as her hands felt under the duvet and touched something square . . .

She pulled out a large box of Maltesers. Maltesers were Cody's favourites.

'Where did you get these, Cody?'

He said nothing, just stared with wide, nervous eyes.

She yanked the duvet right back. A plain white card lay on the sheet. She opened it. In blue biro scribble, it read:

Darling Cody,
    Chocolate for you! Chocolate is the prize for boys who win the game.
    Lots of love,
    Granny xxx

Georgina stood up as if in a dream.

'Bren?' she called, and then half screamed: '*Bren!*'

Cody folded his arms sullenly. 'I *knew* you'd be angry at me.' Georgina was struck by the force of his glare.

Bren came rushing into the room. 'What's wrong?'

Georgina pushed the card into his hand.

He read it, confusion all over his face. 'What is this?' he asked, looking from Georgina to Cody and back again.

'Someone gave him those.' Georgina pointed at the Maltesers. 'An *adult*. An adult wrote that card, Bren.'

'What is this, buddy?' said Bren. 'Is this part of your game?'

Cody looked from his father's bemused but relaxed face to his mother's panic-stricken one. 'Yes,' he said. 'It's part of my game.'

'Oh *come on*, Bren! Did you *read* it?'

Bren studied the card, frowning. 'Calm down, Georgina. I'm not convinced it's an adult's handwriting.'

'You're telling me to be *calm*? Cody, who sent you this?'

'One of the kids at school wrote the card for me,' said Cody. 'I asked them to do it.'

'Why, buddy?' said Bren.

'It's part of my game, I *said*. An important part.'

Bren held up a hand to silence Georgina as she opened her mouth to speak. 'Then where did the Maltesers come from, Cody?'

'I bought them myself. With my own money,' Cody added defiantly. 'My own money that Grandad gave me.'

Bren looked half amused, half sad. What he did not look was afraid. Paradoxically, it would have reassured Georgina to see her own fear reflected on her husband's face.

'Rose always bought him Maltesers.' Bren addressed Georgina in a low voice. 'He wants to pretend he still has a grandmother who buys him presents. Georgina, this is how children deal with things – imagination.'

'You really believe that?'

'And you really believe – what? That they're a gift from beyond the grave?'

Georgina snatched the card out of his hand.

'I won't let you make me out to be the irrational one here! Someone is contacting our son. Who gave you this, Cody?' He drew back from her, and she took him by the arm and pulled him closer, trying to make him see the urgency in her face. 'Tell me!'

'One of the kids at school wrote ... *Ow*, Mam, let go of me!'

'Don't grab his arm like that, Georgina!'

'Cody, I'm sorry.' She let go of him. He backed away rapidly until he was behind his father's legs and continued glaring at her from there. 'But you have to tell me. Who gave you the chocolates?'

'Georgina, let's go downstairs and talk, just the two of us,' said Bren.

'I want my card back,' said Cody loudly.

'Give him the card, Georgina.'

Georgina's eyes widened. She grabbed the box of Maltesers off the bed as well and held them aloft. 'What, and these too? Bren, we don't know who gave these to our child.'

'For God's sake, Georgina.' Bren was stage-whispering in that way adults sometimes did when a child was in the room. 'Obviously we have to discuss this, but not like this!' In his normal voice, he said to Cody, 'Buddy, me and you are going to have a talk about this soon, okay?' Then he turned to Georgina. 'How about, under the circumstances, we let him keep the chocolates and—'

She strode past him onto the landing. They followed her, Cody whining and Bren arguing, but she ignored them both and marched down the stairs.

She'd been right the whole time.

'Georgina, what are you ...'

'No!' Cody wailed. 'Mam, those are mine!'

Bren and Cody were both behind her, protesting, as she opened the bin and poured the Maltesers into it.

'Jesus, Georgina, there was no need to do that.' Bren tried to grab her arm, but she shook him off, shoving the card into the bin too. Purging the house of these tainted items.

'I'm not having him eating those.'

'He's already eaten half of them!'

'They could be poisoned for all we know!'

'Jesus, Georgina, *listen* to yourself.'

Cody was crying now. Georgina crouched in front of him. 'Do you feel sick at all, sweetie? Is your tummy okay?'

'I hate you,' said Cody. But before she could chide him – they tried to discourage that phrase in their house – Bren was there, scooping his son up into his arms.

'It's all right, buddy, it's okay.' He stroked Cody's back. 'There's no need to cry. I'll read you a story. Me and Mam will discuss this tomorrow.' He glared at Georgina over Cody's shoulder. 'When everyone's less upset.'

And they were gone, Cody still crying as Bren carried him up the stairs. Those hiccuping sobs tore at Georgina's heart. But she didn't have time for guilt.

Chocolate is the prize for boys who win the game.

She sank onto the sofa, where she sat like a statue, staring unseeing across the room. How could Bren deny this? It was happening right under his nose.

Chocolate is the prize for boys who win the game.

What game? And who was playing it? How could she protect Cody if she didn't know what she was protecting him from?

23

That evening, after Cody finally fell asleep, Bren and Georgina had a ferocious row. At first he wouldn't talk to her, just strode past her when she tried to speak. He was cleaning the house ostentatiously, keeping deliberately busy so he wouldn't have to look at her.

'Bren, please talk to me.'

He slammed the fridge door.

'Cody cried for half an hour before he fell asleep,' he said in a hard voice. 'I've never seen him so distressed.'

'I'm sorry,' said Georgina, and she was. Hearing Cody cry like that made her feel as if her chest was tearing open. 'But we've got to get answers out of him. He's lying to us.' Bren, tying a knot in a binbag, just shook his head at her. She grabbed his arm. 'Our son is lying to us. How can you be so blind to this?'

He shook her off. 'How can *you* keep insisting on your wild conspiracy theories, frightening your son, when he's told you he's doing it himself?'

Georgina didn't know what to say. If Bren was in a horror movie, he'd be the person denying the existence of monsters even as one tore him apart.

He stamped away to take the rubbish out and came back in with the air of a man who had made an effort to calm down. 'Okay. I shouldn't be so angry at you. I'm sorry you've had such a hard time recently, Georgina, and I'm sorrier than you'll ever know that I added to it.'

'Bren, how many times? This is bigger than you and Emma!'

He looked at her seriously. 'Then I hope you're still planning to go see the therapist on Saturday,' he said. 'Talking about things that are bigger than you and me.'

'*What?*' Her inability to reach him overwhelmed her. 'Have you been listening to a word I'm saying? This is about *Cody*.'

'No, Georgina,' said Bren firmly. 'This is very much about you.'

Bren slept on the sofa that night. He didn't discuss it with Georgina, just brought a duvet and pillow downstairs.

'I'll be awake before Cody,' was all he said.

Georgina's sleep was fractured by vague nightmares. She woke feeling distinctly unrested. Cody was sullen over breakfast and wouldn't kiss her goodbye.

Chocolate is the prize for boys who win the game.

With Bren and Cody gone, Georgina sat in the morning silence and tried to think. What was she supposed to do now? The idea of contacting the police had floated through her mind. But how could she even begin to explain? She had no evidence.

Only the card. And it had ended up in the bin.

She stood up. Bren had taken the bins out last night, hadn't he?

She pulled on a coat and shoes, grabbed a pair of yellow rubber gloves and went out to the front garden.

There was ice melting on the grass and traffic on the road. Georgina approached the wheelie bins self-consciously. At least the people in the passing cars were strangers. She didn't want to think what Bren would say if he saw her rooting through the rubbish.

She lifted the lid of the general bin and, nose wrinkled in distaste, began her search. Her gloved fingers split the taut plastic of the tied black bag. Out spilled used tissues, orange netting, crumpled plastic packaging . . . but no card.

'Morning, Georgina.'

She looked around. Vera, bundled up in a purple scarf that matched her coat, was observing her with interest from behind her round glasses.

'Lose something, did you?'

Georgina stepped away from the bin. 'Yes. My ring. I can't find it.'

The card must be deeper in the rubbish. Goddammit. If she could scrape together enough of an understanding of what was going on to go to the police, it would've been a useful piece of evidence . . .

Vera was still looking at her curiously. Georgina mumbled something about having to get to work and went back inside.

She didn't need the card to picture those scrawled letters. They were burned into her memory.

Chocolate is the prize for boys who win the game.

The rest of the day passed in a daze. At work, Georgina gave customers the wrong change and looked at them blankly when they complained. Driving to Cody's school for pick-up, she nearly crashed twice.

Chocolate is the prize for boys who win the game.

At the school gates, she pretended to listen while Kelly-Anne babbled on and on: 'Have you ever had your eyebrows threaded, Georgina? I *always* have mine done, and they come out so much better . . .' Forced some kind of a smile, a nod.

When the flood of children rushed out, Cody hung back so she couldn't see him. Only when the crowd was dispersing did he trail sulkily over to Georgina. He jerked away when she tried to ruffle his hair.

'Sweetie,' she said, hurt.

'I don't want to talk to you.'

In the car home, Cody sat with arms folded, refusing to answer her questions.

'I'm really sorry I upset you last night, darling,' she said. 'I'm just worried about you, you know that, right?'

'You don't want me to have a new granny,' he said. 'You hate New Granny.'

She caught his eye in the rear-view mirror. 'I thought you said New Granny was pretend.'

Cody looked away. 'She is.'

Bren sent Georgina a long message from work:

> Georgie, I know I could've handled things better last night. But I can't stand back and watch you upset Cody like that. He got the Maltesers for himself and got an older kid to write the note.

That's heartbreaking. You can't get angry at him
for wanting to pretend he still has a grandmother.
I know you don't think you're struggling, but it's
painfully obvious from the outside. Please go to the
appointment I've made for you with the therapist on
Saturday. I know things are complicated between
us right now, but you know I have your best interests at heart.

Georgina read the message briefly and tossed her phone
aside. She didn't have time for this. She was consumed by
fear for Cody.

There was no longer any doubt in her mind. She hadn't
hallucinated the chocolate on her son's face or the handwrit-
ten card. It wasn't paranoia that made her certain Cody was
lying. It was common bloody sense. *He got the Maltesers for
himself and got an older kid to write the note . . .* What *shit*. If Bren
wasn't so damn stubborn, he'd be able to see that for himself.

Perhaps Bren *wanted* her to be unwell, because it would
compress all of this into something clean and simple and easy
to understand. Just poor crazy Georgina again. A one-word
answer, a diagnosis in a doctor's handwriting, something that
could be tied up neatly with a bow, a prescription for medication and a ten-week course of therapy.

You know I have your best interests at heart.

An oddly formal way of signing off. As if he was a stranger
to her rather than the man whose bed she had shared for the
best part of a decade.

Even during the toughest times in their relationship,
Georgina had always felt like Bren was ready to catch her.
It was hard to grasp that she couldn't rely on him now. She

felt as though she were sitting in a familiar old armchair and had leant back comfortably to find the back had disappeared. Where she had always met solid support before, she was now thrown with a jolt into emptiness.

24

The next day Bren took the afternoon off work to bring Cody to the zoo. 'Something to cheer him up.'

It didn't need to be said aloud that Georgina wasn't invited.

Alone in the house, Georgina spread out her college notes and opened up her laptop out of pure habit. Staring at the screen, she realised she wouldn't be able to take in a single word.

Chocolate is the prize for boys who win the game.

You hate New Granny.

She stood up shakily. Her dream of being an art teacher, instead of feeling real and almost tangible as it usually did, seemed far-off and unimportant.

She got out her sketchpad and pencils. Drawing was the only thing that could completely engross her, no matter the circumstances. Once the pencil touched the page, hours slid by.

When she looked up, it was half past five and dark outside.

Bren and Cody would be home soon. Georgina considered calling Bren to ask him to pick up bread and milk, but with things so frayed between them, even this simple domestic request seemed a conversational minefield. Easier to go herself.

She put away her drawing materials and set off to the local shops. Her heeled boots click-clacked loudly in the quiet, making her walk a little faster. But once she turned onto the main road, there were cars, and people bustling about, and Georgina felt safer.

In the corner shop, she picked up milk, bread and one of Cody's favourite chocolate bars. She knew she was trying to buy his affection back, and she knew this wasn't recommended in any of the parenting books, but she didn't care.

You're not the only one who's realised sugary treats are the key to Cody's heart, a little voice whispered nastily in her head.

Georgina felt nauseated. It was too easy, too clichéd: promise a child sweets and they'll lie to their parents for you. She put the bar back, suddenly unable to hold it a moment longer. Paying for the milk and bread quickly, she turned to leave, but bumped straight into someone, nearly knocking them over.

'Oh God, sorry,' said Georgina with a conciliatory cringe, as she looked into a pair of green eyes she recognised, at a pretty, dark-haired woman she knew . . .

'Emma,' she said in shock. Emma, Bren's long-ago girlfriend and recent participant in his extramarital activities, right here in her local shop.

'Georgina.' Emma looked, for the slimmest second, absolutely terrified. Then she plastered a wide Stepford-wife smile across her face. 'How are you?'

The two women looked at each other, frozen.

Georgina had often imagined running into Emma. She had never sought her out – she was not naturally confrontational, and the only person she held responsible for Bren's actions was Bren himself – but she'd scripted it in her head. The perfect cutting one-liner, the devastatingly sharp remark, the flawless retort she would use should her path ever cross Emma's.

She had never imagined she would be paralysed by a lifetime of small talk and social anxiety. She had never imagined her lips would move automatically and reply, 'Good, you?'

'Not bad, not bad.' Emma's smile was fixed, her eyes too wide. She was already moving towards the door, still babbling as she did so, as if pleasantries could construct a protective bubble around her. 'I was really sorry to hear about your mother. Bren told me.'

Georgina's mouth was beginning to catch up with her mind. She did not allow the automatic *thank you* to leave her lips.

'I better hit the road.' Emma backed through the door. 'See you, Georgina.' And with a swish of her dark hair, she was gone.

Georgina stared after her.

What just happened?

Had she just been *civil* to the woman who'd slept with her husband?

And there was something else.

Bren told me.

When the hell had Bren been speaking to Emma about Georgina's mother? He had sworn to her that he'd had no further contact with Emma since that night.

'Wait.' Georgina hurried out of the shop. '*Wait!*'

But Emma was already far up the street, speed-walking away, a slim figure in the distance. She glanced back once before disappearing around a corner.

Georgina stared after her. What had Emma been doing around here in the first place? She lived, as far as Georgina was aware, on the other side of the city.

Georgina walked home quickly. A cat darted across her path, a garage door slammed with a bang, things that would have caused her to start nervously earlier – but now she was driven by a steadily building anger that overrode everything else.

Bren had lied to her. Again. That *bastard*.

The car was parked in the driveway when she arrived at the house. So Bren and Cody were back from their day out.

'Mam!' In all the zoo-related excitement, Cody had forgotten his grudge. He never could hold one for long: beneath his cheekiness and spirit, he was an achingly sweet child, eager to give and receive love. He tumbled into the hall now, holding a stuffed tiger. 'We saw a real tiger at the zoo and it came right up to the glass! And we had sausages and chips.'

'Did you? Sounds lovely.' Georgina held out her arms, and Cody rushed into them. She hugged him hard, his little arms around her neck a balm to all her rage.

'Cody, come with me for a minute, sweetie.' She gripped his hand.

'Where are you going?' asked Bren. Georgina ignored him.

She led Cody outside and over the low wall that separated their garden from Vera's. She rang the doorbell, and Vera answered.

'Hiya, Georgina. Hiya, Cody.' Vera looked tiny in an enormous knitted cardigan. Her round glasses hung on a string around her neck; she put them on and beamed at them both. 'Well this is a nice surprise. Come on in.'

They were ushered into the narrow hall covered in photographs of Vera's grandson. Georgina said in a low voice: 'Vera, would you mind taking Cody for a few minutes? Bren and I need to have a quick chat.'

Cody had gone marching into the kitchen of his own accord. 'Do you have any banana bread, Vera?' he shouted.

'Not today, love,' Vera called, 'but you can have a KitKat and watch some TV with me – how does that sound?' To Georgina she said: 'Of course. Sure he's always welcome.'

'You're a lifesaver, Vera. Thanks.'

Back in her own house, Bren was waiting in the hall. 'Where's Cody?'

'Vera's looking after him for a bit.' Georgina walked past him. 'So you and I can talk.'

They took up stations in their old battleground, the kitchen: him leaning against the counter, her standing by the door. When he looked at her, a kaleidoscope of emotions crossed his face. Anger, guilt, concern, confusion, love.

Georgina understood. She felt the same.

'We do need to talk,' he agreed.

'Yes.' *But not about what you think.* She watched him closely as she continued. 'We need to talk about who I saw in the shops today.'

'What?' Bren blinked at her, wrong-footed. 'What d'you mean? Who?'

'Emma.' She couldn't bring herself to say *your* Emma, though the phrase did jump to her lips. 'Emma Gilligan.'

His head jerked a little, involuntarily. His mouth opened, but no words came out.

When a few moments had passed without Bren managing to speak, Georgina continued. 'And she said the strangest thing.'

'You were talking to her?' Bren's voice came out in a rasp. He was definitely off the offensive now. He coughed, cleared his throat.

'Yes. She offered her sympathies about my mother.' Georgina wanted to sound calm, but she could hear how tightly she was speaking. 'She said you told her all about it. When were you talking to Emma about my mother, Bren?'

One of Bren's hands had begun tapping nervously on his thigh. Georgina continued, keeping her voice as steady as she could. 'Because you told me you haven't spoken to Emma since that night.'

He opened and closed his mouth and looked around the room desperately as though hoping the perfect answer would swoop down and save him.

'Bren. Answer me.'

'I know what you're thinking . . .'

'Do you?' she said coolly.

'It's not . . . Nothing's been going on. A few months after, Emma called me again. She said she wanted to talk. I told her no, no way, I could never see her again and she wasn't to keep calling me. That's all the contact we've had, I *swear*.'

'Why didn't you tell me she'd called?'

Bren looked utterly miserable.

'It was just after Rose died. You were . . . You couldn't even get out of bed. I thought the last thing you needed was to be reminded of . . .'

'You're saying she only called you once?'

'Twice,' he said instantly. 'Twice, and the second time I

got snappy with her. I guess I took my own guilt out on her. I told her your mother had just died, and we had enough on our plate. Basically I told her to get lost. Haven't heard from her since.'

Georgina said nothing, letting the silence drag out.

'What's she doing around here anyway?' Bren muttered.

'That's what I was wondering,' said Georgina evenly. 'She lives on the other side of the city, doesn't she? Rathgar? Rathmines?'

'Rathmines, I think,' said Bren.

'You think? You've never been to her house? She's never been here?'

'No. Georgie, I swear to God. She knows we live in this area, but I never met her around here. It was one time. She wasn't here because of me. Unless ...'

Georgina understood what was unsaid.

'What, you think she's doing her shopping on the other side of the city on the off-chance she might run into you?' Georgina heard the mocking edge that crept into her voice. 'She just fancies you that much, does she?'

Bren looked embarrassed and unhappy.

'Georgina, I don't expect you to believe anything I say right now, but this is the truth. There's nothing going on between us. I haven't seen Emma since that night. *She* called *me*. Her relationship with Christopher was breaking down, and ... I think the break-up made her wonder if she'd made the wrong choice when she left me for Christopher all those years ago. I think it was more nostalgia than anything else. The whole thing was stupid.'

'And you couldn't tell me about it.'

'I thought it was the right call to make at the time. And

140

looking back, honestly, I think I'd still make that call. You were in a bad place, you could barely function, you were—'

'All right.' Georgina got the picture. 'You could've told me about it later.'

Bren shrugged helplessly. 'You're right. I'm sorry. I don't know why I didn't. I just ... Everything was so difficult, and ...'

'And you'd gotten away with it, so you didn't want to risk bringing it up again.'

Bren had nothing to say. Georgina turned away.

She could imagine how the breakdown of a ten-year relationship could make a person look back at their only other serious romance through a rose-tinted lens. It was plausible that Emma, in her loneliness and confusion, had idealised Bren, especially after their stolen night together. It was plausible that Bren hadn't told Georgina about the phone calls because he'd wanted to protect her when she was at her most fragile. It was all so plausible.

But was it the truth?

25

Between his trip to the zoo, the impromptu visit to Vera's, and the KitKat, Cody was overstimulated. He was practically bouncing up and down when Georgina brought him home. When his repeated requests of 'Can I play a game on your phone, Mam? *Please?*' became too much to bear, she gave him her phone – which she had taken out of her pocket with the express purpose of doing some googling and sleuthing – just to shut him up.

With Cody quieted and playing on her phone in his bedroom, Georgina opted to use Bren's MacBook. Her laptop was downstairs and going to get it would mean interacting with Bren. But the MacBook was on their bed and she knew the password.

She settled cross-legged on the mattress, opened Google, and typed the words *ways children deal with grief.* There were 59,400,000 results. Maybe there'd be something on here about kids creating imaginary friends to replace lost loved ones.

In the aftermath of the Bren/Emma saga, Georgina was strangely calm. The anger towards Bren had, oddly, cleared her head. Sitting here now, she felt able to focus on what mattered most – Cody.

She was going to get to the bottom of this. She was going to concentrate.

Though something was niggling at her, a troubling feeling that there was some important detail she had missed ... something someone had said? But no, the half-memory was fading. She couldn't catch it ... It was gone.

Turning her attention back to the computer, she added the words *imaginary friend* to her search.

> It is completely healthy for children to have imaginary friends ...
>   Imaginary friends can help children deal with stress, anxiety or bullying ...

One sentence tugged at her attention.

> Children often imagine they have seen the person who has died. They may search for them, hoping to find them if they look hard enough.

Could this explain Cody's behaviour?

To read more, she had to download the file.

Georgina clicked accept and then opened Bren's download folder. It took her a moment to find the document, but there it was, alongside a number of other files.

Files Bren had downloaded himself.

Files with titles like:

How to win custody – for fathers.
Prove you're the better parent in court!
Child custody: how dads can win.

The disorientation Georgina experienced was not dissimilar to the feeling of waking up in a bed other than her own.

Prove you're the better parent in court!

Her fingertips hovered over the keypad. She glanced at the half-open bedroom door. She would hear Bren coming up the stairs.

She double-clicked.

She read furiously, skimming as fast as she could through pages with sections like 'Dirty Tricks & Tips: How to Get the Upper Hand in Court' and 'Top 5 Strategies a Father Can Use to Win'. She could hear Bren downstairs, moving around in the kitchen. Heart pounding, she opened another document.

In cases of mental illness . . .
When the mother can be proven an unfit parent . . .
Mentally ill or unstable . . .

Georgina tried to make sense of what she was seeing. Theories were forming, but she pushed them away. They belonged to different marriages, different lives. Not to her and Bren. The man who stroked her hair and made her carrot soup when she was sick. Who picked her up when the weight of life threatened to crush her to the floor. The man who said: *Please go to the appointment I've made for you with the therapist . . . you know I have your best interests at heart.*

A small voice in the back of her mind whispered: *Of course, if you do go to that appointment, it'll be on the record that you're currently seeking mental health treatment.*

A louder voice interrupted loyally: *Whatever you're thinking, it's not possible. Bren would never do anything like ... like what this suggests. There has to be an innocent explanation. Such as ...*

But the loud, loyal voice could not, at that very moment, think of any innocent reason Bren would have these resources on his laptop. The small voice came back in, probing, needling: *Once you would've sworn he'd never cheat on you.*

Can be proven an unfit parent ...

Mentally ill ...

She thought of all Bren's encouragement that she seek professional help. The self-doubt he had planted in her head. She fought waves of nausea, disbelief and, worst of all, the urge to run to Bren's arms and beg him to make it better with a nicely packaged explanation, to stroke her hair and tell her everything was fine.

But the words were right there in front of her.

Unfit parent...

Dirty tricks ...

How dads can win...

'Georgina?' Bren was coming up the stairs. Her jump of shock almost knocked the laptop onto the floor. Frantically she began clicking and closing documents, then slammed the computer shut.

'Georgie?' He was on the landing now. Georgina sat back on the bed and tried to look relaxed. Was it obvious her heart was pounding? Her breathing irregular?

'I'm thinking of ordering food,' Bren said, almost apologetically, the tone of a man who knew he was in the doghouse. 'Indian, maybe. Would you like anything?'

'My usual.' Did her voice sound too high? Was it noticeable?

'Korma? Naan bread?'

She nodded, not trusting herself to speak.

'Anything to drink?'

She shook her head. Bren gave her a mournful look, obviously assuming her silence was intended to punish him, and shuffled off. Georgina observed the exaggerated slump of his shoulders, his I-know-I-deserve-it puppy-dog face.

Was it all just an act?

Was he planning on leaving her? And taking Cody?

Unbidden, images came to mind of Bren and Emma, like a terrible highlight reel she was powerless to stop. Clandestine meetings. Elegant hotel rooms. Emma's green eyes. Bren pulling his T-shirt over his head, his taut stomach above Emma's. The two of them curled up in bed afterwards, laughing at Georgina, at her naïvety.

Bren and Emma on a sofa, Cody between them.

Dizzy with it all, Georgina put her head in her hands. Amidst her confused thoughts, she again experienced the strong sense that she was missing something. For a moment, she almost had it, her grasping mind nearly closed on the memory, but . . .

'Georgina, I'm hopping in the shower.' Bren came back into the room. 'If the food gets here, there's cash on the table to tip the driver.'

Georgina made sounds of agreement, but she was on autopilot. Bren was undressing in front of her, grabbing a towel. Bren, her husband, the father of her child.

Men leave their wives for their lovers all the time, the small voice inside her head said. *Spouses file and fight for sole custody all the time.*

Yes, said the loyal part of her, *but . . .*

Yes, but not in my *marriage?* The small voice mocked. *All the time, but never to* me?

There was a roaring in her ears.

Then the small voice said suddenly, clearly: *Leave.*

Her mind went racing ahead of her. She could see herself throwing some clothes in a bag while Bren was in the shower, grabbing Cody, driving to her father's . . .

Crazy, said the loyal-to-Bren voice. *Paranoid. You can't just run out while your husband's in the shower. You have a child, you have a job, you can't . . .*

She stood up, decisive.

There had to be an innocent explanation for the documents on his computer. Bren had failed her in the past, yes, but he was only human. Sleeping with Emma was a very human mistake. This was something else altogether. It couldn't be right. It couldn't. He *wouldn't . . .*

Wouldn't what? Gaslight her? Convince her she was losing her mind? Try to take her son away?

She would ask him. It was that simple. She would ask him tonight, when Cody was asleep.

But somehow she never did manage to ask Bren about the documents that evening. Instead, as they ate their Indian food, as he ruffled Cody's hair and made jokes, she just watched.

Watched, and took note.

26

The next day was a Saturday, but, to Georgina's relief, Bren had been called into work. Grateful for the reprieve, she put Cody into the car and drove to her father's house.

Jimmy didn't comment on his daughter's puffy face or the purple shadows under her eyes, didn't bombard her with questions she wasn't ready to answer. He just welcomed her in and put the kettle on, distracted Cody with stories and allowed Georgina some space.

She lay down on the sofa in the conservatory, mentally exhausted.

'Tea or coffee, Georgie?'

'I'm grand, Dad, thanks. I just want to rest.'

'Cody,' Jimmy turned to his grandson, 'd'you have that super purple whatchamacallit gun with you? How about you and me go out the back and have a game of war?'

Georgina watched through the window as Cody and Jimmy played in the garden, Cody shooting plastic animal bullets around, his grandfather pretending to be mortally wounded. She experienced a rush of appreciation for her father, comforting as a cup of tea on a cold day.

'D'you want to talk to me at all about what's going on?' Jimmy asked her later, when Cody had settled in front of the TV.

Georgina shook her head.

'Well,' he went on, a little gruffly, 'if you ever do want to talk, you know I'm here, don't you?'

'I know, Dad.'

They sat in silence for a while. The only sound was the radio. A news piece on the war in Afghanistan was followed by a debate on abortion. 'Jaysis, Georgina.' Jimmy got to his feet. 'Let's listen to something a bit more cheerful, will we?' He changed the station. 'Now, are you sure you don't want a cup of tea?'

She smiled. 'Really, Dad, I'm fine.'

'Well how about I take Cody to the cinema for the afternoon? Give you a break?'

'Now that,' she said gratefully, 'would be brilliant. Thanks, Dad.'

With Jimmy and Cody gone, Georgina was left alone with her thoughts.

Less than a year ago, her mother would have been here too. Cooking, cracking jokes, making Georgina feel better.

Without her, the big house felt so silent.

What would you have said, Mam? Georgina went into the front room to look at the photo of her newly-wed parents on the mantelpiece. *Did you ever have moments when you lost faith in your marriage?* It was hard to believe. Her parents had always spoken so fondly of the past.

Last May, Georgina and her mother had stood right here and looked at this photo together. 'Oh, we were *happy* back then,' Rose said dreamily. She'd been sick at the time, but not too sick to walk around. 'Did you know that after we were married, we were stuck in a B&B for months? The purchase of our first house had fallen through, and everyone felt sorry for us, but as long as we could be together, we were happy. The B&B was in Drumcondra, on Clonliffe Road, and we used to walk by the canal. Then of course, we ended up buying *this* house, so thank God the first one fell through. Everything happens for a reason, Georgina ...'

Six weeks later, she was gone. Georgina could almost hear her mother's warm voice echo in the room. She missed her so badly it felt like a physical ache.

Before going upstairs, she walked from room to room, ensuring all doors and windows downstairs were securely locked. *Paranoid*, one voice whispered inside her. *Sensible*, another countered. Then she went to her childhood bedroom and lay down.

In the same spot she used to lie as a skinny teenager, worrying about spots and exams and boys, Georgina stared at the ceiling and wondered about Bren.

Last time she'd checked her phone, she had several missed calls from him. This afternoon was the appointment he had booked for her with the therapist. If Georgina hadn't found those documents, she would be there right now, flicking through magazines in the waiting room.

When the mother can be proven an unfit parent ...

Mentally ill or unstable ...

She remembered, unbidden, the figure at the window on their date night, and shivered. A dark thought whispered to her: if Bren has been orchestrating everything, does that mean he got someone to stand at the window? To stare in at you while he was undressing you? To terrify you at your most vulnerable, then tell you it's all in your head?

Georgina flinched from that thought as if it were an angry, buzzing hornet.

She rolled onto her side. After a while, her phone rang. She looked at the screen. Bren, again.

She turned her phone off. A minute later, the house phone began to ring downstairs.

Georgina didn't budge. Bren must have guessed she'd gone to her father's. She lay on the bed and listened.

Ring-ring. Ring-ring.

It rang out. Then, a moment later:

Ring-ring . . .

Someone was determined to get an answer. Maybe it wasn't Bren at all. Maybe it was someone looking for Jimmy. Or – Georgina sat bolt upright – maybe it was Jimmy himself. Maybe he was trying to contact her and, finding her phone off, had called the landline. Maybe something had happened to Cody.

That thought sent her running down the stairs.

She grabbed the phone. 'Hello?'

But the only sound on the other end was a faint crackle.

She looked at the screen. Private number. Bren never had his phone on private.

'Dad? Is that you?'

In the pause that followed, she could hear breathing.

'Who is this?'

The breathing was heavy, distinct. There was movement on the other end. A scratching noise.

And Georgina knew, with absolutely certainty, that this was the same person who had called before and sat without speaking on the line.

'I know you're there,' she said, loud and angry. For a moment she forgot to be afraid. 'Say something.'

Was she imagining things, or did it sound like a woman breathing?

'*Emma?*' she half whispered, disbelieving.

The line went dead.

Georgina put the phone down, a deep feeling of unease gathering beneath her ribcage. She dialled Jimmy's number. 'Hi, Dad, everything okay? You weren't ringing me on the house phone by any chance, were you?'

'No, love. Everything's grand. We're having a great time.'

Georgina made some small talk about 'just checking in' before hanging up.

Who was calling her?

And how had they known she was here?

She went to the front window and peeped through the curtains. A neat front lawn. A quiet suburban street. Nothing to see.

It was at that very moment that the half-memory that had been bothering her returned. Clicking into place.

Rathmines. Emma lived in Rathmines.

Wasn't a café in Rathmines one of the only outlets where Caffrey's toffees could be purchased?

She pulled out her phone and swiftly searched the website. Yes, she'd remembered correctly. Conkers Café, Rathmines.

The golden wrappers in Cody's pockets. The wrapper she had tugged out of the dirt in the icy park.

Georgina stood statue-still, before sinking slowly into a seated position on the stairs. She sat there for a long time.

Rathmines. Was it a connection or coincidence? All Georgina knew was that a cold fear was spreading through her.

Yes, Jimmy bought those sweets. But that didn't mean he was the only person in Dublin who did.

Small details kept coming back to her. All the nights Bren had been working late. The way Cody's eyes had flickered towards him – 'I made her up.' Of course he would lie for his own father.

The thought formed itself, finally, the one she hadn't wanted to face.

Could Cody's 'new granny' be Emma's mother? Was the plan to replace Georgina – a new granny and a new mam too?

27

Stay here, her mind offered. *You don't have to give your dad the details. Just tell him you and Cody need to stay a few days. He won't pry.*

But what about Cody's school stuff? Her laptop, her make-up, her phone charger? What an enormous inconvenience, what a lot of awkwardness and difficulty, and for what? Yes, Bren had some questions to answer, but he was still Bren. It was ridiculous to be *afraid* of going home to her husband.

Wasn't it?

Georgina was still sitting on the stairs, struggling with her thoughts, when Jimmy and Cody got back from the cinema.

'You all right, Georgina?' Jimmy asked, as Cody rushed to hug her.

'Much better.'

She thought about how strong Bren was. How lean, muscular. All those hours at the gym. The arms that wrapped around her during sex and held her afterwards while she fell asleep. Usually those strong arms made her feel, in some deep, primal way, utterly safe. Now . . .

Cody yawned widely.

'I think himself is a bit tired,' said Jimmy. 'Might be time to get him home.'

'I am *not*.' But Cody yawned again, leaning into his mother's arms.

Georgina looked down at her child's perfect, innocent face and felt suddenly clear-eyed. Bren would never hurt their son. It was impossible.

Of course she and Cody could go home. Of course they would be safe.

'Yes, time to go, sweetie,' she said, getting to her feet. She kissed Jimmy goodbye. 'Thanks for everything, Dad.'

Cody was nodding off in the backseat all the way, but Georgina felt anxiously awake and alert.

When they reached the house, however, Bren wasn't there.

'Where's Dad?'

'He must be working late, sweetie.'

It was long after dark. Cody fell asleep on the sofa, and Georgina pulled a blanket over him.

Where *was* Bren? She turned her phone back on. She had no new messages.

Walking into the kitchen, she tried calling him, but his phone was off.

This was most unlike him.

With a growing sense of unease, she went back into the hall, where she stumbled over a bag of rubbish waiting to be carried out to the recycling. And – *dammit* – the wheelie bin had to be put out for collection. That was Bren's job.

She thought of Bren's strong, capable hands. The crook of

his neck where her head fitted so perfectly. He had always seemed so clear to her, so vivid. Now, when she tried to picture him, the image was blurred around the edges, distorted.

How could she ask him about the terrible thoughts she was having? But how could she make any decisions without giving him a chance to defend himself first?

Her head was spinning.

Focus on the small things, one at a time.

Georgina grabbed the bag of recyclables and made for the front door.

Her hand was on the latch when something caused her to hesitate. Perhaps the memory of that anonymous phone call. Maybe she shouldn't go outside. Maybe she should wait until Bren got back.

Don't be ridiculous. You're just taking out the rubbish.

She had enough problems right now without the bin overflowing for the next fortnight. She opened the door.

Cold night air prickled her skin. Briskly she walked across the garden, put the bag into the bin and began to wheel it out to the road.

The night was quiet, almost unnaturally still, as if the whole city was holding its breath. Despite herself, Georgina couldn't help imagining this as a scene in a horror movie. Eerie music getting louder as she got further away from the door. The audience covering their eyes. *Don't go out there! Get back inside!* Unable to watch as Georgina made her way down the short driveway, pulling the wheelie bin behind her . . .

Stop it. She manoeuvred the bin onto the road.

Right. Job done. Time to go back inside.

She paused at the gate and took one last thorough look around. Nobody about. Not even a passer-by in the distance.

Just then, she heard a small sound, like someone suppressing a cough.

Georgina took two steps back, into her own garden. Her eyes flicked up and down the road, but there was no one in sight.

There it was again. A muffled half-cough.

Muffled, but close.

Georgina turned towards her garden and looked at the car.

There couldn't be, she thought numbly.

Very slowly, she lowered herself into a squatting position. Braced on the balls of her feet, she leant forward, hands on the ground, and lowered her head so that her cheek was parallel with the concrete.

Through the narrow gap between the ground and the body of their car, she saw feet. A hunkered-down shape.

There was someone crouched behind her car.

28

How Georgina managed not to cry out in alarm, she did not know. The person on the other side of the car remained completely still.

Very slowly, Georgina pushed her upper body away from the concrete and looked towards the house. She just had to make it inside and close the door . . .

She sprang to her feet and began to run. In the periphery of her vision, she saw the person behind the car straighten up. In her terror, she stumbled and hit the ground. Hard.

Dazed, she scrambled to her feet . . .

And found them standing in front of her, silhouetted against the warm light from the hall, face in shadow.

The figure moved forward, and Georgina flinched back.

A new light fell on their face – *his* face.

Bren's face.

'Bren.' Georgina pressed a hand shakily to her chest. 'Jesus *Christ*. You scared the life out of me!'

He said nothing.

'What the hell were you doing?'

Still, Bren didn't speak. He was swaying slightly.

Then she realised he was drunk. Very drunk. Drunker than she'd seen him in years.

'I was looking through the window,' he slurred. 'To see if you were in.' He looked awful – eyes red-rimmed, skin pasty. 'Didn't want you to see me like this. When you came out, I hid behind the car.'

He took a couple of staggering steps forward. He stank of beer. She stepped back.

'I thought you were at work.'

'Yeah, well … Went for a few afterwards, didn't I?' His bleary eyes focused on her. 'It's your fault anyway,' he said, his voice suddenly clearer and harder. 'And you turned off your phone. So don't give me that look.'

Instinctively, Georgina found herself gauging her chances of dodging past him and into the house. Some primeval part of her brain made the evaluation without being asked and delivered the answer to her consciousness: *Yes, you could make it, just move fast.*

Bren saw her eyes flicker from him to the door. Drunk as he was, understanding crossed his face.

Then his features crumpled. She had never seen him look so hurt.

'Georgina,' he said, making an obvious effort not to slur his words, 'are you *afraid* of me?'

She couldn't answer. For a long moment, neither of them spoke.

Then Bren took several unsteady steps to the side, out of her way. Hands outstretched, palms up.

'Go in if you want,' he said. 'I would never try to stop you. You know that, right? If you want to leave me, I understand. But I don't understand how you could ever think I'd hurt you.'

He looked so unhappy, so sorry.

But the documents on his computer. The toffees that were sold in Rathmines.

'I know what you think.' He swayed slightly where he stood. 'You think I've been seeing Emma.'

Georgina hugged her arms around herself. Somehow they were having this conversation here, in the garden, in the icy cold. But she didn't want to risk breaking the moment by suggesting they move inside. She must proceed with caution.

'Why would I think that?'

Bren looked at her with real anguish. 'I know it looks bad. But I swear to *Christ*, it was just that one night. And I know I should have told you the whole truth from the start, but – *fuck* – I was too much of a coward. I was terrified you'd leave me.'

Georgina said nothing.

Child custody: how dads can win . . .

When the mother can be proven an unfit parent . . .

'I found something on your computer.' The words came pouring out of her mouth; she felt powerless to stop them. 'I wasn't snooping, it was an accident. I downloaded something and when I went into your downloads folder I just stumbled across . . .'

Bren stared at her uncomprehendingly. 'Across what?'

'Some documents about child custody. How fathers can get custody.'

He looked blank. Then slow comprehension spread across his face – and with it, horror.

'Oh, no ... Georgina, *no*. It's not what you're thinking. I was afraid you were going to leave *me*. You were so angry and hurt when you thought I'd just *kissed* someone else ... I kept picturing you learning the whole truth and leaving. So I read up on custody. I downloaded loads of resources, but only skim-read most of them. Some of it was really nasty stuff. I can understand why you would think ... but Georgina, I swear ...' Bren spread his hands imploringly, 'I only wanted to know what the situation would be if you wanted a divorce. What rights I would have to my son. That was all.'

Georgina felt every atom of her body exhale simultaneously. She hadn't realised how much tension she had been holding until that moment.

'I love you, Georgie,' Bren said. 'I'd never leave you. You know that, don't you? I can't picture my life without you.'

The relief was extraordinary. It had all been coincidence, circumstance, miscommunication. Georgina almost fell into Bren's arms right then, beer stink and all. But there was something holding her back.

'So you're telling me you haven't seen Emma in person since that night?'

'No. Georgina ...' Bren trailed off. He hesitated, then spoke with a little more force. 'D'you really want to know the truth about Emma?'

Oh God. When he said it like that, did she?

'Yes,' she said. It was the only answer she could give.

'All right,' he said quietly. 'This is the truth.' He closed his eyes for the duration of one deep breath, opened them again and continued.

'I was bored. It's such a fucking cliché, and I hate to admit it, but I was bored. The seven-year itch or whatever. Before I went out to that stupid reunion, I'd been bored for a while. Bored with my life. Bored with us. Wondering if I'd made the right choice getting married. Wondering if there wasn't still something new out there for me, some new woman or new adventure ...'

Georgina felt an icy sensation spreading through her gut that had nothing to do with the cold.

'You know what I'm talking about. The grass is always greener kind of thing. It's not that I thought I could ever do better than you. It's just that I missed meeting someone new for the first time. That's not something we could ever give each other again. I was curious. I was uncertain about what I wanted. I was sure I loved you, but I wasn't sure I wanted only us, *this*, for the rest of my life ...'

He gestured, implying the unseen bonds that tethered them. There was silence for a moment. Georgina waited. Bren's breath puffed clouds of moisture. The moonlight shone silver on the frosty grass around his feet.

'So I slept with Emma,' he said. 'Because I was selfish. Because I wanted to feel something new. Because I didn't know *what* I wanted. Turns out that half an hour was all it took for me to be sure. Afterwards, I knew all I wanted was you, us. All I wanted was to undo what I'd just done.'

He took two steps back and sat down on the concrete step at their front door.

'I knew you'd sensed something was wrong, so I admitted to kissing her. I agonised over whether to tell you everything.

I already felt guiltier than I'd ever felt in my life. And then, when Rose called to tell us about the diagnosis …'

He buried his face in his hands.

'I thought, okay, I can't tell her the full truth now. Not when her mother's sick. I told myself I was protecting you. But honestly, Georgie … I was glad to have a reason not to tell you everything. It wasn't about protecting you or any of that shit. I was just terrified of losing you. I don't know how I'd get through a day without you, let alone the rest of my life.'

Georgina went over and crouched beside him. She put a hand on his shoulder. He looked up at her in bleary astonishment.

'Okay,' she said. 'Okay.' Translation: *It's not remotely okay. Not right now. But one day, it will be. If we work on it.* 'I believe you.'

'Oh, thank God. I thought … I thought I'd lost … I fucking love you, Georgina, d'you know that? I love you.'

'I know.' She felt a calm certainty she hadn't felt in a long time. 'I know you do.' She stood up, took him by the arm and helped him to his feet. 'Come on, up you get. Let's get you inside before we both freeze to death.'

As Georgina helped Bren through the door, neither of them noticed that someone was watching from across the street.

When the front door closed, the person drew nearer and looked up expectantly. After half a minute, a light came on in the upstairs window. Curtains wide open, Georgina and Bren moved around the bedroom like characters in a silent play. From the street below, their audience of one observed their every move. They watched as Georgina helped Bren onto the bed and covered him with a blanket. As she left the room and returned with a glass of water.

Only when Georgina pulled the curtains shut did the watcher slip away into the dark.

29

'How was your weekend, Georgina?' Kelly-Anne asked her at the school gates.

Oh, it was fine, Kelly-Anne. I thought my husband was setting me up to look crazy so he could steal our son away when he left me for his lover. But it turns out I've just been paranoid all along! Isn't that absolutely hi-LAR-ious?

'Quiet,' Georgina replied. 'Didn't do much. How about you?'

'Well,' began Kelly-Anne, taking a deep breath in preparation for whatever monologue she was about to launch into, and Georgina, knowing feedback would not be necessary, tuned out and let her mind drift back to the weekend's events.

Yesterday morning, she had brought Bren a mug of coffee in bed. 'How're you feeling?'

Bren was abashed. 'I'm all right ... Thanks.' He accepted the coffee without looking at her. 'Georgina ... all that stuff I said about being bored ... Christ, I never meant ...'

'It's okay,' she said, reaching for his hand. 'I'm glad you told me. I'm not saying the explanation excuses what you did, but it helps me make sense of it. Okay?'

He looked up then and leant in to press his forehead against hers.

Kelly-Anne's braying laugh brought Georgina back to the present moment, to the schoolyard with the chalk hopscotch coloured on the concrete.

'It was my birthday on Sunday,' she was saying. 'Mark got me a voucher for this all-day spa experience. Even had the little fish nibbling my feet! Ever tried it?'

'I've never been to a spa,' Georgina said.

'What! At all?' Kelly-Anne seemed dismayed. 'Have you never even had a massage? Georgina, you're missing out!' She tossed her long black hair around her shoulders with a sudden flash of excitement. 'I know! We should go together! Girls' day out.'

Georgina was paying close attention now. She would need to tread carefully to avoid this. 'Sure, sometime,' she said non-committally. But Kelly-Anne was pulling her iPhone out of her pocket and scrolling through her calendar.

'Let's see . . . Maybe a weekday?'

Georgina steeled herself. She wouldn't be swept into spending an entire day with Kelly-Anne. 'I have college and work, Kelly-Anne. I don't have much free time.'

'Oh . . . ' Kelly-Anne looked so disappointed that Georgina felt momentarily guilty, but then the school opened and children began spilling out, and Georgina was saved.

'Maybe some weekend, then, Georgina!' Kelly-Anne called, brightening up already, as they went their separate ways.

Georgina felt somewhat resigned. Perhaps, no matter what

she did, there was no avoiding ending up in a hot tub some-where, cucumber slices on her eyes, listening to Kelly-Anne babble on. The woman was relentless.

At home, Georgina and Cody ate peanut butter and banana sandwiches, and then had 'homework together' time. Afterwards, Cody watched TV while Georgina studied.

'Are you finished yet, Mam? Can we do something fun?'

Georgina closed her laptop. 'Yes, darling.'

The weather was sleeting down outside, a cold grey com-bination of rain and hail, so they stayed indoors and worked on a big art project. Giant sheets of paper, every colour pencil and crayon imaginable, glue, glitter and shiny bau-bles left over from Christmas were all used for their abstract creation. When it was completed, they hung it up in the kitchen, then curled up in front of the TV, warm under the knitted blanket.

'I love you, sweetie,' Georgina said, stroking Cody's hair. 'You know that, don't you? I love you more than anything else in the world.'

Cody took this proclamation in his stride, with the ease of a child who has always been adored. 'I love you too,' he said, eyes fixed on the screen.

Eventually Georgina got to her feet. She could lie here forever with her son, but there were chores to be done.

She walked out to the hall, picked up this morning's unopened post and carried it into the kitchen. Brushing some glitter off the table, she sat down. There was a bill she'd been expecting and a white envelope she hadn't.

Curious, she opened the white envelope first. The page she slid out was stamped with a familiar logo, that of their phone provider. With it came a hand-written note:

I'm a mother too. Nina.

Georgina recalled the morning she'd rung the telecom company and asked a woman named Nina for a record of calls made to their landline.

She sat quite still, not looking at the page. The image of Cody on the sofa, phone pressed against his ear, giggling away, was still conjured easily in her mind. If he really had been on the phone to someone, she was about to find out.

She gazed across the room. There was rain on the window. The sky outside was somewhere between a threatening iron-grey and black.

Just read it, she thought briskly. Put this idea out of your head once and for all.

She looked down at the page.

The list was short. Georgina and Bren barely used the landline.

So who had received a long call from a private number on Saturday 9 January? *Duration: 13 minutes.*

Saturday the ninth. Her mind flew back through the dates, mental calculations concluding that yes, that was the same evening Cody had sat on the sofa, chatting into the phone. The same day the long pauses in his conversation had struck Georgina as eerily real.

The previous day, another phone call:

Incoming call – private number. Duration: 4 minutes.

She recalled coming in from the garden to find Cody crouching behind the sofa, phone to his ear. How he said into the receiver: 'She found me.'

She remembered the call to the house the night before, nobody speaking when she answered, how she had thought someone was trying to scare her.

But their intention hadn't been to frighten her. They hadn't been calling for Georgina at all.

They'd been trying to reach Cody.

Her hands had begun to shake. The page trembled in front of her. She placed it down on the table.

Duration: 13 minutes.

She and Bren had stood there watching and arguing while someone had been on the phone to their son.

The stick-figure drawings. The sweet wrappers. *I said she could be New Granny.*

She grabbed her phone.

'Hey,' Bren answered pleasantly. 'I'm stuck at work, but I'll try and get out in the next half—'

'Bren,' she interrupted him in a rush. 'I just saw our phone records for the past month. You know all those times Cody was pretending to be on the phone? *There was actually someone on the line.*'

There was a moment of silence. Then: 'You're serious, Georgina?'

'Yes. Bren, somebody's been calling and having long conversations with him.'

She kept her voice low, although she was sure Cody couldn't hear her from the sofa in the front room. The TV was still playing loudly.

Bren was asking, 'Have you got the number there in front of you?'

'The caller ID was withheld.' She looked at the page. 'I can send you a photo.'

'No, I believe you. I'm just trying to make sense of it. Could it have been one of his friends calling from their parents' phone?'

Georgina put a fingertip on the words: *January 9 . . . 13 minutes . . .* 'The calls correlate with the times Cody told us he was talking to his new granny.'

'Okay,' said Bren. 'Okay. I'm going to come straight home.'

Georgina's gaze was drawn back to the square of the kitchen window, where the figure had stood staring in at her. With the phone records in front of her and silence all around, she no longer believed she had imagined it.

'I want to get Cody out of this house and bring him somewhere safe. My dad will let us stay for a few days.'

'Wait for me to get home at least, and we can discuss it. I'm leaving work now . . .'

She heard a soft *thud* from outside, like feet on concrete. Bren was still speaking. 'We can sit down, talk to Cody . . .'

Georgina lowered the phone. She sat absolutely still. She strained her ears.

For a moment, she thought she'd imagined it.

Then she heard the heavy sound of the side gate rattling.

Georgina raised the phone to her ear. 'Bren,' she breathed. 'There's someone at the house.'

'*What?*'

'I can hear them moving around outside.' She pushed the chair back and got to her feet, keeping her eyes trained on the kitchen window. 'Call the Guards.'

'Okay. I'll have to put you on hold. Don't hang up.'

The line went silent. Georgina began to back out of the kitchen, without taking her eyes off the window. She would grab Cody, get him upstairs . . .

Then she heard a giggle behind her.

She turned towards the hall, and froze.

Cody was standing at the front door, his back to her. He

was peering through the letter box. As if in response to someone on the other side, he nodded his dark head and let out another hushed, secretive giggle.

'Cody!' Georgina screamed, and he whirled around. She rushed forward to drag him away. 'Who were you talking to?'

Cody was silent. Georgina, clutching his arm, was too frightened at first to approach the door. Gathering her courage, she released Cody and edged close enough to peer through the peephole. But whoever was there had ducked out of sight.

'Cody, who was out there?'

'No one.'

She grabbed him by the hand and pulled him up the stairs. Bren was on the line again. 'Georgie, the Guards are on their way. Are you there? I'm racing home right now.'

'We're here.' Georgina marched Cody into her bedroom. Fuelled by terror and adrenaline, she began tossing clothes into an overnight bag.

'Where are we going, Mam?'

'Grandad's,' said Georgina shortly. 'Sit on the bed, Cody, where I can see you – no, don't you *dare*! Don't you *dare* leave my sight!'

Cody sank down onto the bed with uncharacteristic obedience. Perhaps he picked up on how tense Georgina was, how close to snapping like a dry twig.

Bren stayed on the phone the whole way home. He arrived before the police. Georgina had never felt so glad to see him.

'There's nobody out there now,' he said. His eyes fell on the packed bags.

'Bren, I'm not staying here after this. I've never been so frightened in my life.'

'Well, we have to wait for the Guards anyway.' Bren folded her in his arms. 'We'll see what they have to say.'

Two members of the Guards, the Irish police force, arrived within five minutes: a man and a woman. But the ensuing conversation did not go as Georgina had envisioned. Neither of the Guards seemed convinced that receiving calls from an unknown number was cause for panic. Nor did they seem compelled by Georgina's story. It didn't help that Cody claimed his mother was making everything up.

'I was playing a pretend game,' he insisted.

The two police officers looked at each other, then at Georgina.

'There was somebody in my garden,' she said. 'I heard them.'

'But you didn't actually see the intruder?'

She looked guiltily at Bren. She wished she'd thought quicker, crept to the window and looked out to see who was at the door without alerting Cody to her presence.

'No. I just grabbed my son and took him upstairs.'

'Well,' said the Guards before they left, 'we've registered the incident. Get in touch if anything further happens.'

When the door closed behind them, Georgina turned to Bren, expecting him to say something about her overactive imagination. But Bren was studying the phone records, a deep line between his eyes. He went over to crouch in front of Cody.

'If you lie to the police, you get in very serious trouble. Did you know that, buddy?'

'Not if you're a kid,' said Cody calmly. 'Kids don't get in trouble with the police, not properly. Kids can lie to the police.'

There was a silence.

'Where did you learn that, Cody?'

Hesitancy flickered across Cody's face.

'Um,' he said. 'I think I heard it at school.'

'Really.' Bren looked straight into his eyes. 'Did a grown-up tell you that?'

'No.' But Cody had turned faintly pink.

Bren straightened up, frowning. Georgina pulled him aside.

'I'm not staying here,' she said. 'I don't feel safe. That's the end of it.'

Bren wasn't looking at her. His eyes were still on his son's flushed, obstinate face.

'Actually,' he said, 'I'm starting to agree with you.'

The wave of relief she experienced was so strong that Georgina felt unsteady.

'Mine and Cody's bags are already packed,' she said. 'Grab whatever you need for work tomorrow. I'll call my dad.'

While Bren was packing his things, Georgina tried one more time. 'Cody, that was New Granny at the door, wasn't it? What was she saying to you?'

But Cody, lower lip protruding, remained stubbornly silent.

30

That night, in her childhood bedroom, Georgina unpacked the few bits and pieces she'd hurriedly jammed into a bag in the rush from their house. Cody's knitted blanket. Some of his T-shirts, jeans.

'I'll get the spare room cleared out,' her father said. 'So the three of yous won't have to be crammed in here.' Jimmy had allowed some clutter to accumulate in the spare room – an exercise machine Georgina had bought him eight years ago that he never used, the boxes of Rose's old things.

'We're fine here.' Georgina was happy to be anywhere but her own home.

'And we'll only be here a few days,' offered Bren. 'Just till we get the kitchen fixed.'

Georgina's father was under the impression that a broken pipe and flooded kitchen was the reason they were staying with him. The last thing they wanted was to worry Jimmy.

'Stay as long as you want, Georgie,' he was saying now. 'Sure I love having yous here.'

That made something in Georgina's chest tug sadly. 'Thanks, Dad.'

It felt strange, the following day, to drop Cody off at school as usual. Bren and Georgina both took the day off work, telling Jimmy it was to pop over to the house and see how the repairs were coming along.

At their house, they spent the afternoon searching for clues, brainstorming theories and making calls to Cody's classmates' parents into which they tried to weave leading questions about whether any of their children were behaving strangely. They came up with nothing.

They collected Cody from school together and brought him back to Jimmy's, where Jimmy tried to engage Bren in conversation about the fictional burst pipe. 'How're the repairs coming along? I've got a number for a good plumber if you need one.'

'Thanks, Jimmy, but I've already found someone. They said it's a big job and it'll take a few days.'

When Bren left the room, Jimmy said to Georgina, 'Just be careful you're not getting ripped off, love. I could always pop around and have a look myself, if you want.'

Georgina knew that while her father would never say so aloud, he did not consider Bren sufficiently masculine to be trusted to keep an eye on dodgy workmen.

'Thanks, Dad, but really, we've got it under control.'

After clearing the table, she followed Bren upstairs to her old bedroom, where they could speak freely.

'I hate lying to my dad,' she said.

175

Downstairs, she could hear the shouts and laughter of Cody and Jimmy playing together.

Bren flopped onto his back on the bed, and Georgina lay down beside him. He put an arm absent-mindedly around her.

'We're going to get to the bottom of this. Whatever's going on, we'll figure it out.'

She nodded.

'I was thinking,' he continued. 'What if it's an elaborate burglary scheme? Kids often know the alarm code to houses, right? Or where their parents keep the keys. If you took the time to befriend a child, they could get you inside . . . '

Georgina was shaking her head.

'We're not rich,' she said flatly, speaking into his shoulder. 'Who would go to that much trouble to rob us?'

'I suppose. It was just a thought.'

They were both quiet for a while. Then Georgina said, 'Bren – it couldn't be anything to do with Emma, could it?'

The side of Bren's face she could see reddened. 'Definitely not. She's not the type to go all *Fatal Attraction* on us.'

'You're sure?'

'I'm sure.'

There was a pause, during which Bren scratched his chin and appeared to contemplate something.

'Here's a thought,' he said slowly. 'Cody's drawings of his new granny . . . didn't they look a bit like Vera?'

'Vera?' Georgina almost laughed. 'I don't think they did. Anyway, Vera has nothing to do with this.'

'How can you be so sure?'

'Because we know Vera! Anyway, whoever was talking to Cody outside the door ran off within seconds. When I looked out, there was no one there. Vera wouldn't be able to move that fast.'

'Fair enough,' said Bren tiredly. 'I'm just thinking aloud. The only other theory I keep coming back to is the awful thought that someone's targeting Cody ... Grooming him ...'

The word *paedophile* hung in the air between them.

'But an old woman?' Georgina was grateful the profile didn't fit. 'It doesn't make sense.'

Bren made a *hmm* sound in his throat. 'It's unusual, but it does happen.' She didn't want to hear this, but he kept talking. 'And people who target children sometimes use women to lure them in. Like those human trafficking groups that get older women to act helpful and motherly and say they'll get the girls waitressing jobs ...'

Georgina stiffened against his side. 'Yes, but it couldn't be something like that. There's no human trafficking in Ireland, is there? And anyway,' she barrelled on, not waiting for an answer, 'those people don't target kids like Cody, who are safe and cosseted and loved. They target vulnerable kids, lost kids, kids who won't be missed.'

Saying those words brought an unexpected lump to her throat. She swallowed it back down. Downstairs, they could hear Cody shouting at his grandfather. 'Bang bang, got you! Bang bang, you're dead!'

'Whoever he's in contact with,' said Georgina, 'it's someone he likes and trusts. He's lying to us to protect them.'

She could feel the tension in Bren's body. 'If only I'd listened to you from the beginning,' he said. 'If only I hadn't been such a stubborn prick, then we'd have a head start on solving this. I'm so sorry ...'

'I know. You said.' Georgina wasn't interested in his self-admonishments. 'Let's just focus our energy on figuring this out.'

While she didn't feel ready to accept his apologies, she did feel an overwhelming relief that she and Bren were back on the same team.

Later that day, they tried interrogating their son once more. But Cody refused to reveal the identity of his visitor. He refused to admit there had been anyone at the door at all.

'I was just looking out, Mam.'

'Just looking out the letter box?'

He shrugged. Georgina exchanged a glance with Bren, who was standing with arms folded. She was cross-legged on the carpet in front of Cody, who was perched on the edge of the bed, legs swinging sulkily back and forth.

'Sweetie,' she said, forcing herself to remain calm, 'will you please tell us who was on the other side of the door?'

Cody was silent.

'Was it New Granny?'

Nothing.

'Was it the same person who gave you the Maltesers?' Bren interjected. 'The lollipop?'

'No.' Cody addressed his father. 'There was nobody at the door. Mam is making it up.'

Georgina's fingernails dug into her palms. 'Cody, Dad's seen the phone records too. We both know there was really someone on the phone.'

Cody averted his gaze sullenly. 'I was just talking to my friend from school.'

'Which friend?'

'Umm . . . Patrick.'

Bren said lightly, 'Oh, okay. I'll just call Patrick's parents then and check.'

Cody looked over sharply at his father. Georgina could almost hear the mechanics of his brain whirring as he considered his bluff.

'Actually, no,' he decided. 'It wasn't Patrick.'

'Who was it then, Cody?' Georgina pushed. 'I promise I won't get cross.'

'I don't remember.'

'You don't *remember* who you were on the phone to?' She wanted to cry with frustration and fear. 'Cody, that's enough! You're lying, and it's not allowed. If you tell me the truth, I won't be angry at all. But if you don't, I'll . . . I'll . . . '

She groped around in her mind for a punishment severe enough.

'I'll take away the Mega-Power Purple Slinger Machine Gun.'

Cody's features began to crumple, first in disbelief, then denial. 'You won't. You can't! Grandad gave it to me! It's mine!'

'If you want to keep it,' said Bren, 'answer our questions.'

Cody was in the bargaining stage. 'Please, Mam, I'll be good.'

'Just tell us who was on the phone.'

'I told you! One of my friends from school, but I don't remember who.' He'd reached anger now. 'You can't take my Mega-Power Purple Slinger Machine Gun! You can't!'

'We can and we will, if you don't tell us the truth,' said Bren.

'I hate you!' Cody shouted, before bursting into tears and racing out of the room.

Georgina got to her feet and turned to Bren helplessly. She hadn't flinched at the 'I hate you'. She'd heard it before, and it was always taken back by clingy, cuddly Cody at bedtime: 'I love you, Mam. I didn't mean to be mean.' She didn't feel hurt by Cody's outbursts. She felt only one thing: afraid.

Who was her son lying for?

31

They decided to try a different approach. The following afternoon, Bren took Cody out for a treat, to see if he would open up.

Cody had got over the trauma of having his favourite toy taken away. He was now in a good mood, enjoying the novelty of staying at his grandfather's and being taken out on a school night.

'Dad's bringing me to the cinema and to Eddie Rocket's. I'm going to get a milkshake!'

'And if this doesn't work?' Georgina asked Bren quietly, as Cody put on his coat.

'We'll figure it out.' Bren squeezed her hand. 'I promise.'

From the doorway, Georgina watched them drive away, a hard knot in her stomach.

'You all right, love?' Jimmy was looking at her shrewdly. 'You seem a bit stressed.'

'This business with the kitchen has my head wrecked,

Dad.' She hated lying, but what else could she do? The truth was too dark and murky and tangled. And the fact that Rose's name was caught up in it? It was too much, too heavy.

'I'm going to sit down and watch a bit of telly,' Jimmy said. 'D'you want to join me?'

'Maybe in a bit, Dad. I'm going to go upstairs and get some studying done.'

This was another lie. There was no way on earth Georgina could focus on her studies now. She did go upstairs, sitting at her old school desk and taking out a notepad and pen, but the heading she wrote across the top of the page read:

CLUES.

Underneath, she began to jot down words and phrases.

Park. Lollipop.
She said she was my granny.
Toffee wrappers. Drawings. Phone calls.
Maltesers. Card.
Chocolate is the prize for boys who win the game.
Someone following me home. Someone at the door.
Someone watching the house??

She sat back and read over it, but the longer she stared at the page, the less sense she could make of it all.

Her phone beeped. A message from Bren.

> **No luck so far. He just keeps denying everything.**
> **We raised one stubborn kid.**

Georgina sighed. Distantly she could hear the sound of the TV, and the phone ringing. She imagined Jimmy heaving himself up with a sigh, ambling into the hall to chat to whoever was calling, then grabbing some crackers and cheese from the kitchen before returning to his armchair. He was undoubtedly watching some awful political chat show, arguing with the guests and hosts, addressing the screen as if they could hear him: 'Ah get up out of that, would you, you dirty liar! Are you going to let him get away with that?'

Georgina felt a strong nostalgia for her childhood days: Jimmy shouting at the TV, Rose rolling her eyes in the background, the smell of a roast cooking. Perhaps she should join him, for a while, for old times' sake.

Through the ceiling, she heard the muffled 'Hello?' as he answered the phone. She stood, stretched and yawned. After tidying up the desk, she walked out onto the landing. She was at the top of the stairs when she heard a shout below. Followed by a heavy thud.

'Dad?' she called, hurrying her footsteps. She went quickly down the stairs and into the hall.

What she saw struck her with a jolt of shock so forceful it felt like a physical blow.

Jimmy was on his knees on the carpet, gasping for breath. One of his hands was clawing uselessly at his chest, the other scrabbling for the phone, which had fallen just out of reach. His eyes turned to her in mute appeal.

'*Dad!*'

Georgina ran to him, breathless with terror. Eyes bulging, Jimmy clutched at her arm. For a moment it seemed as if speech was beyond him, but then he managed to croak, 'Call . . . an ambulance. I think . . . my heart . . . '

And he collapsed. It was a tableau that would remain in Georgina's memory forever: her father face down on the floor, the fallen phone on the carpet beside him.

32

The chairs in the waiting room were an alarmingly bright shade of orange. Combined with the dark green of the walls, it made Georgina's stomach churn.

'Hey.' Bren appeared in the doorway with a paper cup of instant coffee from the hospital cafeteria. Georgina accepted it gratefully and took a sip. The bitter taste was strange on her tongue. She had cut out coffee many years ago, replacing it with green tea and chamomile. Right now, though, anything to keep her awake.

'Why don't you come home?' Bren asked her. 'They said he's stable.'

She shook her head. 'I want to be here when he wakes up.'

Bren sat down and put an arm around her. She rested her head on his shoulder. They were silent in each other's company for a while.

'I better go,' he said eventually. 'It's late, and Cody's still at Kelly-Anne's.'

'I know.' Georgina nodded. 'It was very good of her to take him. Thank her for me, will you?'

'I will.' Bren got to his feet.

'Here.' She took out the keys to Jimmy's house. 'You are bringing him back to my dad's, right?'

There was too much pressing in on her, from too many angles. She couldn't concentrate on being there for her father if she didn't know Cody was safe.

Bren took the keys and put them in his pocket. 'Don't worry, Georgie. All three of us are staying safely at Jimmy's until we figure out what's going on.'

He leant down towards her – hesitated for half a beat – and kissed her on the forehead. Then he straightened up, and they looked into each other's tired, raw faces.

'Hell of a time for this to happen,' he said.

'I know,' she said. 'I know.'

Hours crept by. Georgina must have dozed off on the ugly orange chairs at some point. She woke to a nurse gently shaking her. It was getting light outside.

'Your father's awake.' The nurse had a kind voice. 'He was asking for you. It's not official visiting hours, but come on through just for a moment.'

Disorientated, Georgina sat up and ruffled a hand through her hair. Her mouth tasted sticky, of saliva and stale coffee. She needed to brush her teeth.

'Thank you,' she said to the nurse.

Jimmy's hospital window faced the sunrise, and the pale shell-pink light illuminated his grey, tired face. The doctors had called it a mild heart attack, which seemed an oxymoron to Georgina's layperson's ears. Still, the word 'mild' had left her hopeful, and she was shocked to see how bad he looked: his face drained of colour, wires and tubes connecting him to ominous machines.

'Georgie,' he said wearily. 'My great girl. Saved my life, you did.'

She sat down on the chair beside the bed and took his hand. His fingers squeezed weakly back.

'Sorry,' he said, the words seeming to cost him a great effort, 'if I gave you ... a bit of a fright.'

He winked at her through his tiredness, and Georgina almost smiled.

'Oh Dad,' she said. 'Don't you go anywhere on me now.'

'I won't,' he promised. But he sounded so tired.

They didn't talk much. She assured him that Cody was okay, that he had spent the evening at his friend Patrick's house, and that Bren would give him a suitable-for-seven-year-olds version of what had happened.

'I'll leave you to rest, Dad,' she said presently. 'You sound exhausted.'

'I'm knackered,' he said. 'Heart attacks really take it out of you, what?'

Reluctantly, she laughed. Encouraged, Jimmy slipped further into his comedic role.

'Poor aul' Georgie,' he said, 'what a week. First the pipe in your kitchen goes, then your old dad!'

Georgina felt cold. But she showed some of her teeth in what she hoped was a passable imitation of a smile. Jimmy seemed appeased.

As she got to her feet to leave, a thought occurred to her.

'Who were you on the phone to, Dad?'

Jimmy's head twitched towards her. 'What?'

'Who were you on the phone to when you collapsed?'

He just stared at her. Perhaps he couldn't remember the moments before the heart attack.

'I just wanted to call them and let them know you're okay,' Georgina explained. 'They must have got the fright of their lives.'

'Ah,' said Jimmy. 'Yes. It was Billy, as it happens. Don't worry, I got the nurse to send him a text for me.'

'You're way ahead of me.' Georgina kissed him on the forehead before she left. 'I love you, Dad.'

33

'Is Grandad going to die?'

Georgina, tidying the breakfast table, looked up. Cody was standing in the middle of the room, school bag on his back, face puckered with worry.

'No, sweetie. Grandad's doing much better. The doctors say he can come home soon.'

Cody didn't look reassured. Since Rose's passing, he understood death. There was still a frown line between his eyes as he left with Bren for school. Georgina watched him trail down the long driveway, a small figure with hunched shoulders, and her heart ached.

When they had driven away, she went upstairs to her father's bedroom. Jimmy had asked her to collect him some clothes, and also to 'bring me in some decent food, would you? This hospital muck is awful.'

She hadn't lied to Cody. Jimmy had looked greatly improved on her last visit. The colour was returning to his face. He'd been sitting up in bed, reading the broadsheet newspaper.

'Bring me in a bottle of red wine too, would you?' he'd added.

'You're joking, Dad,' Georgina had replied uncertainly.

'I'm not. Something good. South African, maybe.'

She rapped him gently on the knuckles with the pen she was holding. 'The doctors say you have to lay off the wine. And the steak.'

Jimmy only huffed. 'A life without wine and steak? That's not a life worth living.'

Georgina didn't find his grave humour quite as funny as he did.

In the bedroom her parents had once shared, she found and folded her father's clothes and packed them into an overnight bag. T-shirts, fresh socks, underwear ... What else had he asked for? 'A couple of good books.'

She began to scan the bookshelves. They were mostly her mother's old books. Marian Keyes, Maeve Binchy ... Jimmy wouldn't be caught reading those.

Was that a James Patterson on the bottom shelf? She crouched down and slid out *Along Came a Spider*.

As she did so, she glimpsed a narrow box at the back of the shelf, jammed behind the row of dusty books. Curiosity captured, she pulled out several paperbacks, piling them on the carpet, and manoeuvred it out.

The box was filled with small and forgotten things – paper clips, old postage stamps, pens – the kind of objects that gathered in the corners of long-lived-in houses.

It also contained a number of loose photographs, in faded sepias and greys.

Emotion welled in her chest as she picked up a black-and-white snapshot of her mother, taken before Georgina was born. The grey tones rendered Rose's auburn hair the colour of soot, and she stood with the awkwardness of a person unused to being in front of a camera, but none of this detracted from her beauty.

Georgina glanced at and impatiently put aside several photos of people she didn't know, before finding one of her parents on their wedding day. They were looking at each other with such love it brought a lump to her throat.

She flicked eagerly through the rest. Jimmy was younger in these, enormously tall even then, but lanky rather than broad, and utterly baby-faced. Just a teenager. Seventeen, eighteen at most. And there was Jimmy's brother Billy, immediately distinguishable at any age due to his enormous nose and ears, looking dizzyingly young.

There was a teenage girl in the next photo, standing beside Jimmy. Georgina didn't recognise her. She was boyishly skinny, with short black hair and freckles.

Georgina put that photo down and picked up another.

The black-haired girl was in this one too. Just her and Jimmy, side by side. Georgina guessed their ages at around sixteen. The girl was wearing a checked dress. Georgina wondered who she was. A relative? A neighbour?

She continued sifting through the photos. There was a hilarious one of her uncle Billy as a baby – he had the huge ears even then – which made her laugh aloud. She snapped a photo of it on her phone to send to Bren.

And there were several more of Jimmy with the skinny black-haired girl. In one, she was smiling, revealing teeth that would have braces snapped onto them straight away by any parent nowadays. Despite this, Georgina thought she had a certain prettiness, with her deep dimples and mischievous grin.

There were some later photos, too. Jimmy, Billy and a wide and varied cast of family members. Georgina noticed that the girl with the black hair didn't feature in any of those.

She slipped the photo of her parents on their wedding day into her purse. She also took one of Jimmy and the black-haired girl, making a mental note to ask him who she was.

Then she tidied away the rest of the pictures, replaced the box and put the books back on the shelf.

When she arrived at the hospital, Jimmy was asleep.

Georgina left the bag of clothes in his wardrobe, placed the paperback book on his bedside table and arranged some flowers she'd bought in the gift shop by his bed. She propped the photo of Jimmy and Rose on their wedding day against the vase. After a moment's thought, she placed the photo of Jimmy and the black-haired girl there too. She would ask him about it next time.

'Love you, Dad,' she whispered, kissing him feather-light on the forehead before she left. He didn't stir.

Back at the house, Georgina, Cody and Bren were still sleeping in one bed in Georgina's old bedroom. This wasn't the most comfortable arrangement: it got too warm, and Cody kicked in his sleep. But after everything that had happened over the past few days, Georgina was grateful to fall asleep with her husband and son within arm's reach. At least they had this place of refuge, somewhere they could be safe.

34

If they were going to be staying at her father's a while longer, they needed more clothes. The next day, Georgina pulled into the driveway of her own small red-brick house.

'Why are we here?' Cody wanted to know.

'Just to collect some things.'

She watched him closely. Did being here remind him of New Granny? But his attention was already turning back to the book he was reading.

'Can I stay in the car, Mam?'

'I'd rather you didn't.'

'Please?'

'Okay, okay.' She'd be in and out faster without him.

On the doorstep, she paused and looked around the street. At Cody reading in the car, at Vera's neat lawn and Anthony's overgrown one, at the Brazilian couple leaving number 24 hand-in-hand.

All familiar. All quiet.

Once upstairs, she packed quickly, glancing out of the window often to reassure herself that Cody was still safe in the car. She'd rather not linger here.

She tossed some socks and pyjamas into the suitcase. What about her laptop, textbooks? After a pause, she packed them. She should take them, even though college work had been at the bottom of her priority list these last few days. Classes had started again last week, but with everything that had been going on, she hadn't made it to a single one.

Downstairs, she turned on the alarm and went out to the front garden.

The car door was open. The backseat was empty.

'Cody?' Georgina looked around wildly. For one heart-stopping moment, he was nowhere to be seen.

Then she spotted him in the next garden. Talking to Vera.

'Cody!' She slammed the car door shut and went striding over the wall to join them. 'I told you to stay in the car.'

'Ah, hiya, Georgina.' Vera smiled at her, all permed curls and round glasses. 'Nothing to worry about. He was right here with me.'

Vera's front door was open. A warm smell of baking wafted out.

'Can we go in for a scone?' Cody asked Georgina.

'Not today, sweetie. We've got to visit Grandad in hospital.'

'Oh, come on in for a minute, Georgina,' said Vera. 'I have something for you.'

'For me?'

Vera, already on her way inside, didn't hear. Cody was close behind.

With a sigh, Georgina followed, glancing at her watch.

Vera's house felt stuffy, overly warm. In the narrow hallway,

Georgina shrugged off her coat, looking at the photos of little Sean, Vera's grandson. Sean as a newborn. Sean on his first birthday. Sean just months ago, big for his age, beaming, right before his parents took him away to Australia.

'Will you have a scone, Georgina?' Vera called from the kitchen.

'No thank you.' Georgina followed them down the narrow hall. Cody was already at the kitchen table, stuffing a scone into his mouth, crumbs and jam on his face. Every surface was covered in knick-knacks, ornaments, doilies. The tea cosy was a knitted owl that reminded Georgina irresistibly of Vera herself.

'Take some for your dad, then,' said Vera. 'How's he doing?'

'Better, thanks,' said Georgina. 'Actually, we can't stay long. We've got to go see him.'

'Of course.' Vera put some scones into an old biscuit tin and closed the lid. 'Just come into the front room with me a minute. I've something for you.'

'Okay.' Georgina surreptitiously checked her watch again. Cody stayed in the kitchen, eating his jam and scone with great concentration, as Vera led Georgina into the front room.

Vera's sitting room was faintly musty. The net curtains kept most of the sunlight out, making the room feel stale somehow. Vera was fiddling with a box, muttering, 'I'm sure it's in here somewhere.'

'What is it?' Georgina asked.

Vera didn't answer. Georgina turned to look at yet another photo of baby Sean on the wall, with his mother, Lorraine. Despite her impatience to get going, she felt a stab of sympathy for Vera, clear and sharp. Her only child and grandchild gone, half a world away.

There was a noise behind her.

'Vera?' Georgina turned around.

Vera was standing there holding out a cosy home-knitted jumper.

'I've been knitting loads lately,' she said, 'but I've nobody to give my stuff to. I used to always knit things for Lorraine, and I still knit in her size, without thinking. You're about the same size, aren't you? Would you wear this?'

Georgina *was* about the same size as Vera's daughter, but she'd never be caught wearing this misshapen jumper in public. Still, she thought, looking at Vera's round, friendly face, she could always wear it at home.

'Thanks, Vera,' she said, taking it from her. 'I'll definitely get some use out of it.'

Vera beamed. Georgina gestured towards the photo of Lorraine and baby Sean.

'You must really miss them.'

Vera turned towards the photo. She looked at it in silence. Then she turned back to Georgina.

'Do you want to know something I haven't told anyone?'

Georgina hesitated. The air in the room was thick, too warm. She felt a sudden pulse of anxiety. What was Vera about to tell her?

'Okay,' she said uncertainly.

Vera's back was to the window, her face in shadow.

'I don't really miss them at all,' she said.

Georgina stood still, the knitted jumper in her hands. She had no idea how to respond. What on earth did Vera mean by that?

There was a long pause. Dust motes floated in a thin beam of afternoon sun. It seemed as if Vera was about to say something else – then Cody came barging into the room.

'Can I watch TV?' He licked jam from the corners of his mouth.

'No. We're going now,' Georgina said firmly, taking a step back. 'Thanks for the jumper and the scones, Vera. We've got to get to the hospital.'

'Come back soon,' Vera said, waving as they left.

As they got into the car, Georgina pondered Vera's words. *I don't really miss them at all.* What a strange thing to say. She climbed into the driver's seat and looked back at Cody. 'Got your seat belt on, kiddo?'

'Yep.'

She placed the tin of scones on the passenger seat and put her phone to her ear to call her father. Jimmy answered on the third ring. 'Hello?'

'Hi, Dad. Cody and I are on our way over to the hospital now. Can we bring you anything?'

'What?' Jimmy sounded flustered. 'Listen, don't bother coming over now, Georgina. It's not a good time.'

Georgina frowned. It sounded like he was outside. Was that *singing* in the background? Cheering?

'Where are you? That doesn't sound like—'

Jimmy spoke over her. 'What do you *want*, Georgina?'

His tone was uncharacteristically curt, and Georgina, confused, said, 'I called to ask if you wanted me to bring you anything. And if you got the things I left for you last time – the flowers, the photos . . .'

And then Jimmy shouted at her. A real, angry shout.

'*You* left those photos there?'

Georgina flinched and held the phone away from her ear. Jimmy never yelled at her. 'Dad? I'm sorry if I upset you . . .'

'How dare you go through my private things!' Jimmy

bellowed. Georgina, holding the phone at a distance, could hear every word. Cody was watching in alarm. 'How dare you! Learn to mind your own business—'

Georgina's eyes blurred with tears. 'I'm sorry! Dad, I didn't mean—'

'Don't come to visit me today.' Jimmy was no longer shouting, but his tone was harsh. 'I need to be by myself.'

She heard, again, the sound of a rowdy crowd in the background. That definitely wasn't the hospital. 'But Dad, where *are* you?'

He hung up.

35

After Jimmy hung up, Georgina sat in the car, stunned, tears wet on her cheeks. What had just happened?

'Is Grandad angry, Mam?'

'Yes, sweetie.' But why? She tried calling again, but Jimmy had turned his phone off.

'Mam?'

'One moment, darling.'

The knot in her stomach tightening further, she called the hospital. The nurse who answered was sympathetic and perhaps more forthcoming with details than was strictly allowed.

'Your father checked himself out against our advice. The doctor told him – *I* told him – but he wouldn't listen. He seemed,' she went on gently, 'quite agitated.'

'Do you know why?'

'I'm afraid not. I just know that he was determined he wouldn't stay in the hospital a moment longer.'

Georgina thanked her and hung up. What had she done wrong? Why had Jimmy shouted at her like that?

Cody reached forward from the backseat and put a small hand on her shoulder.

'He won't stay angry, Mam. Just say sorry loads of times. If you say it enough, it works. That's what I do when you're angry at me.'

Georgina made a sound that was half-laugh, half-sob. 'Oh, is that your strategy, kiddo? I've got you sussed now.'

But her hand found Cody's and squeezed it tight.

'Let's go over it again,' said Bren. 'He was angry at you for going through his stuff?'

It was the evening, and they were in Jimmy's front room. Georgina kept expecting him to arrive home. She stood by the window, looking down the long garden towards the street, watching cars pass by.

She nodded. 'Even though he'd *asked* me to go through his stuff. It doesn't make sense.'

'It's not like Jimmy at all,' Bren agreed. 'D'you think the heart attack could be affecting his behaviour?'

'I thought it was strokes that did that. But maybe ... He didn't sound like himself at all. The nurse used the word "agitated".'

'Maybe it's his medication.'

Georgina felt a pang of fear at the thought of Jimmy out there somewhere, alone, confused ...

'Where do you think he is tonight? A hotel? He doesn't even have his car.'

'I'm sure he's okay,' said Bren gently.

'You don't know that.' She thought back to her father's

words. What was it exactly he had said? *Mind your own business . . .*

'It must have been the photos that got him so upset,' she said. 'Maybe they brought back bad memories.'

'Thought you said they were just family photos? Him and Rose at their wedding?'

'And one of him with this girl I've never seen before . . . Wait there.'

Georgina hurried upstairs. She returned with a sepia-toned photo of Jimmy and the black-haired girl standing side-by-side, smiling, squinting in the sunlight.

'Maybe she's an ex-girlfriend,' she said as Bren studied it.

'And what, all these years later, seeing her still stirs up such dramatic emotions?' Bren looked unconvinced. 'Must have been some break-up.'

Georgina took the photo back.

'Okay, maybe it wasn't a break-up.' She looked down at Jimmy's youthful features, at the girl's crooked teeth and dimpled grin. 'Maybe something else happened. Maybe she died.'

She was expecting Bren to shoot this theory down, but he was listening, so she continued.

'In tragic circumstances. Then all these years later, he wakes up and finds her photo by his hospital bed . . . no explanation . . .'

'I guess it's possible,' Bren said. 'Then seeing her photo unexpectedly after all these years could trigger a huge reaction. But we don't *know*, Georgie,' he added, in a brisker tone. 'Maybe that's total fiction. Maybe it's simply that his medication's made his brain foggy.'

'But the pain in his voice . . .' Georgina had heard it. Under the anger. 'I've never heard my dad like that before.'

You *left those photos there? . . . How dare you . . .*

She walked away to stand in the middle of the room.

'If it *was* something like that, and I left that photograph by his bed . . . ' Guilt flooded her.

'You're beating yourself up over nothing, Georgie,' said Bren. 'This is just a theory, and until we find your dad, we've no way of knowing if it's true. There's nobody else we can ask.'

She turned around.

'Actually,' she said, 'there is.'

Billy. The boy with the big ears in the photographs was an ageing man now. The early-onset Alzheimer's had taken so much away from him, so many years that could have been good, well lived. He was Jimmy's younger brother; he looked a decade older.

But Billy had memories. They were jumbled and confused, but he had them. Jimmy, who visited him often, had told her once that sometimes Billy brought up things from decades ago as if they had happened last week.

She looked at the photo of her teenage father. 'If Jimmy was sixteen or seventeen,' she said, 'Billy would have been eleven or twelve.'

'Billy,' said Bren thoughtfully. 'There's an idea. You think he might have the memory buried somewhere?'

'I don't know. But I think it's worth a try.'

36

The grounds of Billy's nursing home were spacious and beautiful, lined with trees. The building sat squat in the middle, ugly and square and grey. A concrete box with a lock on the front door.

Bren and Georgina had both taken the day off. After dropping Cody at school, they'd driven here. Georgina had purple circles under her eyes. She'd slept fitfully, hoping all night that her dad would return. He hadn't.

The care assistant who let them in, a warm-faced Filipina woman in her forties, smiled a genuine smile when they asked for William McGrath.

'Ah, Billy!' she said. 'Billy is one of my favourite residents. This way.'

They followed her down a broad corridor. The walls were painted a faded yellow, which might have been bright once. A glance into the TV room showed Georgina a group of residents sitting in front of a television too small for any but those seated closest to see. Most were just staring into space. For all the care assistant's warmth, this was a gloomy place, and Georgina felt guilt for allowing her visits to her uncle to tail off. While she and Billy had never been close, and Jimmy had told her repeatedly that Billy was confused by other visitors, right now those sounded like weak excuses for not doing the right thing.

'We've moved Billy to a new room recently,' the nurse was saying. 'He had trouble with the stairs and he doesn't like the lift . . .'

Georgina was relieved to find that Billy's new room was large, with wide windows overlooking the grounds, and walls a pleasant shade of cream that had clearly been painted more recently than those in the corridor.

Billy was sitting in an armchair. He looked up when they entered, but only for a moment, before he resumed staring at the cream wall. His ears and nose still stuck out, the ears almost comically prominent, but there was nothing else comical about his appearance. His face was sunken. His eyes a fading blue. He looked far older than his years, far older than the last time Georgina had seen him.

'How are we doing today, Billy?' The kind-hearted care assistant fussed around him, adjusting his pillows. 'Your niece has come to see you, isn't that nice?'

Georgina sat down facing Billy. Bren remained standing, discomfort written all over his face.

'Billy, it's me, Georgina,' she said cautiously. 'How are you doing?'

Billy looked past her as if she wasn't there. Didn't recognise her. Didn't even seem to see her. Jesus, thought Georgina, please don't let this happen to me someday.

'He has good days and bad days,' the carer said quietly.

Georgina wanted to cry. She'd known Billy was deteriorating, but she hadn't realised he was this far gone.

The carer gave Billy another big smile, then said to Bren and Georgina, 'I'll be down the hall if you need me,' and left.

Georgina, exchanging a nervous glance with Bren, took the photo of Jimmy and the black-haired girl from her pocket.

'Do you know who I am, Billy?' she asked, keeping the photo flat on her lap. 'I'm Georgina. Jimmy's daughter.'

No response. His eyes looked past her, his face a waxy mask. Feeling an unpleasant twisting in her stomach, Georgina held the photograph up.

'Do you recognise this girl, Billy?'

Something flickered across Billy's face. A reaction.

'Billy?' Georgina glanced at Bren. He was leaning forward; he'd seen it too. 'Do you remember her?'

Billy's head jerked, very slightly, from side to side, but his eyes were focused on the photograph. He recognised the girl, Georgina was sure of it. His hands, which had been resting on his knees, began clenching and unclenching.

'Was she Jimmy's girlfriend?' Georgina held the photograph closer to him. 'Did something happen to her?'

Whatever memories were being stirred up were not pleasant ones. Billy jerked his head faster, mumbling something unintelligible. His face was growing blotchy; his distress palpable.

'Jesus,' Bren muttered.

The cruelty of what she was doing struck Georgina. She lowered the photograph, experiencing a wave of sickening guilt.

'This is pointless,' she mouthed at Bren, and to Billy she said, 'I'm sorry, Billy. Shush now. Everything's okay.'

His mumblings trailed off. There was a moment of complete silence in which Georgina wondered what to do next and Bren stared miserably down at his shoes.

Then Billy opened his mouth and said, 'They sent her to the laundries.'

Bren's head snapped up. Georgina froze.

The laundries. Those words had a particular meaning in Ireland. A meaning heavy with the country's ugliest history.

Billy went on, as if someone was disagreeing with him. 'They lied and said they didn't, but they did, they *did*.'

'Who?' Georgina said urgently. 'Who lied?'

Billy's eyes screwed shut, then snapped open again. He shook his head.

'What was her name?'

But Billy would answer nothing else. He mumbled, 'They sent her to the laundries' once more, then felt silent, still shaking his head from side to side.

'Okay,' said Bren quietly. 'Georgina, I think we should . . .'

There were voices in the corridor. Footsteps growing closer. Georgina stowed the photograph in her pocket.

'Yeah,' she replied. It was only when her vision blurred that she realised she was crying. She wiped her face with the back of her hand. 'All right.'

Billy had retreated into himself. Georgina reached out and touched his arm. 'I'm so sorry, Billy,' she said, tears spilling down her face now.

Billy just stared dully back.

They sent her to the laundries.

The Magdalene laundries and the mother-and-baby homes. Everyone in Ireland was familiar with the dark legacy of those institutions. Their ghosts howled up and down the country.

To get pregnant outside marriage was, in those days, an unspeakable disgrace. Shameful. Hushed up. Girls whose bellies began to swell mysteriously disappeared 'to go stay with family down the country'. Everyone knew where they really went. The mother-and-baby homes were run by nuns. The babies were taken away, often by pressure or coercion, to be given to proper married couples for adoption. The mothers, some of them just children themselves, laboured for their keep; hard manual work. Some returned to their communities afterwards, red-lettered. Others – often those whose families wouldn't have them back – went on to the Magdalene laundries, those asylums where the nuns kept 'fallen women' away from the rest of society. Some never left.

They lied and said they didn't, but they did, they did.

Bren and Georgina sat in the car outside the nursing home, stupefied. Georgina couldn't comprehend this. She had been imagining wild stories in which the girl had drowned. Been murdered.

Anything but this.

'So my dad . . .' she said slowly, then trailed off.

Bren said nothing, letting her get there on her own.

'My dad got his girlfriend pregnant? And sent to one of those places?'

Bren kept his words measured. 'Until we speak to Jimmy, there's no way to know for sure. Billy could have been confused. We don't have all the information.'

'Yes, but what do *you* think?' Georgina was watching him closely.

Bren said nothing, but his face was full of compassion. Georgina felt a lump rise in her throat. She turned away, facing out the car window, looking across the spacious grounds of the nursing home.

Then she made a small, compulsive movement as the next penny dropped.

'If that *is* what happened, then . . . ' she swallowed hard, 'that means I have a half-brother or sister out there somewhere.'

Bren had obviously got there already and been waiting for her to catch up.

'It's possible you do,' he said, his tone careful. 'It's possible you don't. Even if she was Jimmy's girlfriend, she might not have been pregnant. Sometimes women were sent to the laundries just because they'd been sexually active. Sometimes just because it was *suspected* they'd been sexually active.'

This did not make Georgina feel better. It made her want to cry.

'And if she *was* pregnant,' Bren added, 'she might have miscarried.'

Bits of information Georgina had learnt about the Magdalene laundries over the years flitted through her mind. Had she heard somewhere that the last one had only closed in the *nineties*? Was that possible? She'd read an article once about an adoptee who had come back to Ireland from America looking for her birth mother and was horrified to find her still labouring in the Magdalene laundry where she had spent her entire adult life. Working six days a week, every week, for no pay. Trapped, exhausted, institutionalised. Aged beyond her years by the hard labour, hard life.

Was that what had happened to the mischievous–looking

girl in the photograph, with her freckled face and dimpled smile?

'I can't breathe,' said Georgina. 'I can't breathe.'

She clambered out of the car, gulping cold air into her lungs, feeling claustrophobic even beneath the broad grey sky.

37

The next morning Georgina woke with a sick feeling in her stomach. It was a damp, drizzly day, the city was shrouded in a veil of misty rain, and her father was still missing.

Bren took another day off work to be with her. 'They can manage without me,' he said. It was clear to Georgina that he wanted to help but wasn't sure how. He hovered on the sidelines as she walked around her parents' house, from room to room, looking at the paintings and furniture her mother had chosen.

Had Rose known that Jimmy had got another woman pregnant, long ago? Well, a girl. A teenager.

They sent her to the laundries.

It was now two full days that Jimmy had been missing. Georgina sent pleading messages to his phone.

> **Dad, please write back! Just let me know you're okay.**

So far, no response.

Whatever he might've done, he was her father. She loved him. And he was out there somewhere, unwell and alone . . .

She was so worried she couldn't think straight.

Bren was in proactive mode. He called Kelly-Anne and asked her if she could take Cody for a couple of hours after school, then called all the local hospitals looking for Jimmy and the police to report him missing. When none of that worked, he tried calling hotels.

'D'you have a man staying with you at the moment called James McGrath? No, I understand you can't give out guests' details, but if you could just . . . *Shit*.'

'What are you going to do? Call every hotel in Ireland?' Georgina sat in an armchair by the window, staring out at the grey rain.

Did she have a brother or sister somewhere in the world? Many Irish babies during that time had been adopted by wealthy American families. If her half-sibling existed at all, that was likely where they had ended up. Were they in Ireland or America? Were they alive or dead?

She had not slept properly in forty-eight hours, and her eyelids felt heavy. Her head drooped onto her shoulder . . . Before she knew it, Bren was shaking her awake.

'Sorry for waking you when you're so exhausted, but I'm going to collect Cody and I didn't want you to wake up alone.' He handed her a keep-cup of coffee. 'Here. I thought you might want a coffee for once.'

'I'll come with you. Has my dad been in touch?'

But she knew the answer already from the look on his face.

Bren drove. Georgina, in the passenger seat, sipped her

coffee. Bren was right. She *was* exhausted, physically and emotionally.

They sent her to the laundries.

Dipped headlights flashed by and the tarmac glistened as they drove across the city through the hazy rain.

On the way, Georgina and Bren stopped off briefly at their own house to collect some things. As they left, Georgina bumped into Anthony, wearing a warm coat and hat and the air of a man headed somewhere important.

'Georgina, how're you?' Anthony greeted her. 'Have yous been away somewhere?'

'Well, sort of. We've been staying with my father. He hasn't been well.'

'Sorry to hear that.'

Anthony waited until Bren, passing with a suitcase, was out of earshot before adding, 'And how're you, Georgina, really? Haven't climbed into anyone's garden lately, have you?'

Despite everything, she found herself smiling. 'No,' she said. 'I haven't. How're you, Anthony?'

'Well, actually' – Anthony visibly swelled with pride – 'I'm just on my way to collect Lily. My son lets me take her out on my own now. Give himself and the missus a bit of a break, y'know,' he added importantly.

'Anthony, that's great!' Georgina was sincere. The happiness Anthony radiated was powerful enough to lift her out of her own messy life for a moment.

'Yeah,' he said, eyes bright, 'yeah, it is. Next week, I'm taking her to the pet shop to choose a new rabbit. It'll be Lily's rabbit, but it'll live with me. Just to make life easier for everyone.'

Georgina hid her smile. 'So where are the two of you going today?'

'I'm taking her to Howth. She loves looking at the boats. The weather's meant to clear up, and there's a market on there at the moment – stalls and that – good for the kiddies. Jaysis,' Anthony glanced at his watch, 'I'd better run. See you later, Georgina.'

He was holding himself differently, she thought as she watched him walk off. He looked taller.

'Georgina!' Bren called from the car. 'Come on.'

Realising she had been standing there in the rain, Georgina shook herself and hurried to the car.

On the drive to Kelly-Anne's, Georgina felt slightly off. She had underestimated just how unused to coffee she was. The caffeine was jittering unpleasantly through her body, and she knew that once it faded, she would feel utterly exhausted again.

Bren turned into the estate. 'Which house is theirs?' All these houses looked the same to Georgina, but Kelly-Anne's was identifiable by the tall spiral bushes in the front garden.

Bren pulled in alongside those gaudy sculpted bushes, and Georgina jumped out of the car. The air was thick with a drizzle that felt somehow claustrophobic. Pulling her coat over her head like a hood, she hurried up to the semi-shelter of the doorway and rang the bell.

Mark answered. He was a stocky, muscular man with tattooed arms, handsome enough to cause a stir at the school gates on the rare occasions he turned up to collect Patrick instead of Kelly-Anne. 'Georgina,' he said in surprise.

'Hiya, Mark.'

He stood blinking at her, rather stupidly, apparently lost for words. Georgina didn't understand why he looked so baffled.

'We're here to collect Cody?' She ended the sentence as a question in response to the mystified expression on Mark's face.

'Well, there's been some sort of mix-up then,' he said apologetically. 'Cody's already been collected.'

Georgina would never forget this moment. The soft rain falling around her, the sharp, cold smell of winter. The stab of tension in her gut that brought it all into high definition.

'What do you mean, Cody's been collected?'

Mark looked awkward. 'Sorry, Georgina,' he said. 'I assumed you knew she was picking him up.'

Bren arrived at her shoulder. 'How's things, Mark?' he asked, and a feeling of unreality swept over Georgina.

'What do you *mean*, he's been collected?' she said again – only this time she shouted it, in a voice like glass shattering, and both Mark and Bren turned to stare. 'What *she*? Who collected my son?'

Mark's eyes were round pools of startled blue.

'His grandmother,' he said.

38

Georgina stared at Mark in frozen horror.

'What did you say?'

'His grandmother collected him,' Mark repeated. 'About half an hour ago.'

Georgina didn't say anything more. She couldn't. It had suddenly stopped raining. The silence, in the wake of the soft patter of raindrops, in the wake of the words Mark had just uttered, seemed deafening.

'Is this some sort of joke?' Bren said.

Clearly Mark thought he'd stumbled into some complicated family drama. 'Sorry,' he mumbled. 'I assumed it was okay . . . Cody was so happy to see her. She's your mother, right, Bren?'

'Cody doesn't have a grandmother,' said Georgina. Then, because Mark was gawking uncomprehendingly at her, she said it louder. '*He doesn't have a grandmother!*'

'Who took him?' Bren's voice was getting louder and louder. 'Who did you allow to take my son?'

Mark took a half-step back. 'Bren, Georgina, I . . .' He trailed off, looking around for assistance.

As if summoned, Kelly-Anne swooped into the hall. 'Georgina, Bren, hi!' Her smile disappeared as she saw their faces. 'Oh God, what's happened? It's not your dad, is it, Georgina?'

Bren said desperately, 'We're here to collect Cody,' as if hopeful that Kelly-Anne would reveal this had all been a practical joke.

'But his grandmother's already picked him up!' said Kelly-Anne. 'Was she not supposed to?'

Bren opened his mouth and closed it again. His face had gone blank. Mark looked absolutely terrified.

'Kelly-Anne.' Georgina's voice shook. 'That wasn't his grandmother. Cody's grandmothers are both dead.'

Kelly-Anne's mouth fell open. She appeared, for once, to be lost for words.

'We have to call the police.' Georgina fumbled in her bag. She touched tissues, a glasses case – where was her phone? She upended the bag, contents scattering on the carpet, but oh God, *her phone wasn't there.*

She swayed, and might have fallen if Kelly-Anne hadn't come to life. She moved forward and caught Georgina's arm. With her free hand, Kelly-Anne dialled three digits and pressed her own iPhone to her ear.

'Police,' she said clearly, in response to the tinny voice on the other end, and then, to Georgina, 'You're saying Cody's been abducted, is that right?'

Wordless, Georgina could only nod. Kelly-Anne was speaking to the Guards, firm and capable: 'A little boy, seven years old . . . From 26 Grange Road . . . 'Bout half an hour ago . . . I didn't see the kidnapper, I was at the shops, but my husband did. Hang on.'

Kelly-Anne shoved the phone at a shell-shocked Mark. 'Tell them everything you remember about this woman,' she instructed. Then, to Georgina and Bren, 'Do you know who she is? Why she took Cody?'

'She's his new—' Bren began, and broke off. 'Jesus fucking Christ,' he said instead. 'This can't be happening.'

Mark was speaking into the phone, panicked. 'Grey hair, sort of short . . . I didn't notice, did I? The kid said she was his grandmother! He *wanted* to go with her!' Behind him, seven-year-old Patrick peered around the kitchen door, listening in. When Georgina noticed him, he ducked out of sight.

Kelly-Anne was looking at her keenly. Georgina tried to speak, but her breaths were coming faster and faster. 'Someone's been stalking him,' she managed to say, but her chest was tightening, *she couldn't breathe* . . .

She was only half aware of being steered into a mono-chrome kitchen and pushed into a white leather chair.

'Drink this.' Kelly-Anne handed her a glass of water. 'Now. Did you say somebody's been *stalking* Cody?'

Georgina nodded. 'An old woman.' She sipped some water, though she was trembling so violently her teeth chinked off the glass. 'She said she wanted to be his new grandmother.'

'His new *grandmother*?' Kelly-Anne's perfectly shaped eye-brows shot up. She took the glass from Georgina.

'I thought it was a game at first,' Georgina explained. 'But then I started finding sweets, notes . . .'

Mark and Bren followed them into the room. Bren was the palest Georgina had ever seen a person.

'The cops want to talk to you, Georgina.' Mark held the

phone out to her. 'Can you remember what Cody was wearing?'

She tried to take it, but it fell from her shaking hand. Bren picked it up and held it to her ear.

'Orange hoodie, green T-shirt with dinosaurs on it, blue jeans, red shoes, black coat,' she recited. Cody had complained that the T-shirt was babyish. She could see him at the breakfast table that morning, eating Rice Krispies and doodling on the newspaper.

That morning. Just hours ago.

She let out a moan. The Guard on the other end of the phone was asking something, but Georgina pressed a hand to her mouth, stumbled over to the glossy sink and retched.

Kelly-Anne stroked her back. 'They'll find him, Georgina,' she said. 'In over ninety per cent of child abduction cases the kid's retrieved unharmed. In the UK, a child is reported missing every three minutes, and they're almost always brought home safe and sound.'

Straightening up, Georgina looked at her. Kelly-Anne shrugged.

'I watch a lot of true crime. You pick stuff up.'

Bren was saying something to the police. Georgina caught Cody's hair and eye colour. Kelly-Anne went on, 'In the majority of cases, it turns out to be someone the kid knows. It's almost always a family member. Can you think of any relative who might have taken Cody?'

Georgina shook her head.

Kelly-Anne called her son over. 'Patrick, did *you* see the lady who took Cody?'

Patrick nodded, frightened eyes darting from his mother to Georgina.

'And did you recognise the lady, P? Ever seen her before?'

He shook his head.

'Had Cody ever told you about her before?'

'Yes,' admitted Patrick. He was tearful now. 'Cody told me he had a new granny. He said she was picking him up but that it was a secret.'

Georgina's whole body was trembling, but Kelly-Anne remained composed.

'Did Cody tell you where his new granny was taking him?'

'For a fun day out.' Patrick started crying noisily. 'Cody didn't know where they were going, but he said his new granny promised she'd buy him candyfloss. He said it was a special treat because he won the game.'

The world swam. Georgina slid down onto the tiled floor and closed her eyes. The inside of her lids was an explosion of orange against black.

Chocolate is the prize for boys who win the game.

As if from far away, she heard Kelly-Anne saying to Patrick: 'Shush, sweetheart, it's not your fault.' And to Mark, 'Did this woman have a car?'

'I didn't see.'

'She had a car.' Patrick sniffed. 'It was blue. I saw them get into it.'

Georgina opened her eyes. The world was shivery and inconsistent around her. She wanted to give in and collapse and sob. But that wouldn't help Cody.

She tried to collect her scattered thoughts.

What was it Kelly-Anne had said?

Almost always a family member . . .

Something clicked in Georgina's brain.

Jimmy's disappearing act. His odd behaviour.

'My dad.' She grabbed the kitchen counter and pulled herself to her feet. She felt unsteady. 'I think my dad . . .'

She looked towards Bren, but he was still on the phone to the police. Kelly-Anne looked up sharply. 'You think your dad's involved? Isn't he in hospital?'

'He ran away from the hospital.' Georgina gripped the counter to keep from falling over. 'He's been acting strange. He wouldn't tell me where he was going . . .'

Kelly-Anne straightened up too. 'Do you think Cody and this woman are with your father?'

'I don't know. I don't even know where my father is! I called him, but he just shouted at me. Then he turned his phone off . . .'

She was aware that she was babbling, but Kelly-Anne was listening closely.

'You spoke to him on the phone?'

Georgina nodded. 'Two days ago.'

'Did he let anything slip that hinted at his location?'

'Nothing.' Georgina clenched her fists until her nails bit into her palms. How was she ever going to find her dad . . . find Cody . . .

'Focus,' Kelly-Anne urged her. 'During the phone call, was there any detail you noticed? Anything at all?'

Georgina tried to think back. Jimmy had been shouting at her. *Learn to mind your own business*, he'd said. And she hadn't been able to hear him well because . . . Because in the background . . .

'It was noisy,' she recalled. 'He was somewhere outside. There was chanting and cheering . . . sounded like sports fans.'

'Donegal versus Meath,' said Kelly-Anne immediately.

'What?'

'Two days ago? There was a game at Croke Park. Donegal against Meath.'

Croke Park was a huge sports stadium in Drumcondra, near Dublin's city centre.

'You're sure?'

'I got Mark tickets,' said Kelly-Anne. 'So maybe your dad's staying somewhere in that area?'

Georgina felt hopeless. Why would Jimmy be staying there? He had no friends or family in Drumcondra that she was aware of. She couldn't make sense of it. Drumcondra ...

Then she heard her mother's voice. *We were stuck in a B&B for months ... but as long as we could be together, we were happy ... in Drumcondra, on Clonliffe Road ...*

She straightened up. It wasn't much to go on, but – it was a connection. Was it possible that was where he had gone?

'Georgina?' said Kelly-Anne.

'I think I might know where he's staying.' Acting on pure instinct, Georgina moved towards the door.

'Georgina!' Bren stopped her. 'Where are you going? The police are almost here.'

Georgina turned to Kelly-Anne. 'What do I do?'

'You think you know where your dad is?' Kelly-Anne clarified. 'And you think Cody might be with him?'

'*Jimmy?*' Bren said disbelievingly.

Georgina nodded.

'Obviously, you *should* wait here for the police,' said Kelly-Anne. 'But if you think you might know where your son is ...' She trailed off, but her eyes held Georgina's, and her expression said: *If I were you, I'd go right now.*

Georgina turned to Bren, who was white-faced and ter-rified. 'I have to try. Talk to the police for me. Tell them everything. Tell them I've gone to Drumcondra. Once I figure out the exact address, I'll let you know – that is, if he's even there.'

'Georgina, what the fuck are you talking about?'

She felt sorry for Bren, whose fear and confusion and dishevelled hair made him seem like a little boy himself. But she had no time for pause. She stepped over the scattered contents of her handbag in the hall, stooping only to grab her keys, and ran to the car.

'*Georgina!*' Bren yelled after her. But she was already in the driver's seat, slamming the door.

If she could track down her father, maybe she could find her son.

39

Georgina sped through the city streets. Her phone was in the car mount where she'd left it. She tried calling Jimmy, but each call went, as she'd predicted, to voicemail.

'God*dammit,* Dad!' she yelled as she shot through a red light. There was a furious blare of car horns, but Georgina barely heard it. She had to go fast. *She had to find her son.*

Her phone rang. She felt a desperate hope that it would be her dad, telling her Cody was with him, and safe.

But it was Bren.

'The Guards are here. They want to talk to you.'

A policeman's amplified voice filled the car. Where was she going? Why had she reported her son missing if she believed he was with his grandfather?

Georgina tried to explain, tripping over her words, struggling to focus on the road. It occurred to her, with a wave of fear, that the police might be taking this less seriously because she had rushed after Jimmy. Did that give them the impression of a family drama, a *domestic*, something less than police business?

Tears stung her eyes. The road blurred, and the car swerved dangerously. She forced herself to focus. Wrapping her car around a lamppost wouldn't help Cody.

'I have to hang up,' she said thickly. 'I'm going to crash.'

Maybe she was stupid to think her dad was hiding out in this particular B&B just because he had an emotional link to it. But he had sounded so distraught, so lost, on the phone. She could imagine him gravitating towards another familiar place, somewhere with comforting memories.

Do you think Cody and this woman are with your father? Kelly-Anne had asked.

Georgina didn't know. But his disappearance was too much of a coincidence. With every passing second she grew more certain that Jimmy had some connection to whatever was going on.

Pieces swirled in her brain. Pieces she should have put together sooner.

Jimmy on the floor, clutching his chest, the phone on the carpet beside him.

His explosive anger: *You left those photos there?*

The grainy images of the skinny girl with the short black hair. Always standing beside Jimmy. Vanished from the later photos.

They sent her to the laundries.

Georgina stepped down on the accelerator. One thing she was sure of: her father had been lying to her. *This time, Dad, you're going to tell me the truth.*

Evening was creeping dark and shadowy across the city. Streetlights were flickering into life as she reached the red-brick roads of Drumcondra. Croke Park stadium dominated the skyline. She drove slowly, looking for street signs . . .

Yes. This was Clonliffe Road.

And there – a sign for a B&B.

Georgina swerved into the first available spot. She grabbed her phone, leapt out of the car and ran.

The B&B in which her newly-wed parents had once stayed was number 44. It had ivy growing up the walls, a large square reading VACANCIES in one window and a sense of having not been renovated for decades. The mousy-haired woman sitting at the front desk, reading a romance novel, looked up with alarm when Georgina raced into the foyer. 'Can I help you?'

'I'm looking for a man called Jimmy McGrath.' Georgina was aware she was speaking too loudly. 'Or James. James McGrath.'

The mousy-haired woman looked askance. 'I'm sorry,' she said, 'but we can't give out our guests' details.'

Georgina forced herself to lower her voice. 'He's my dad, and I'm really worried about him.' Knowing that under other circumstances this lie would make her feel miserably guilty, she added, 'He's got Alzheimer's, see, and he's run off.'

The woman was wavering.

'Please,' said Georgina. 'He's a danger to himself. He thinks it's 1972.'

With a sigh, the woman put down her paperback and stood up.

'We're not supposed to do this. But . . .'

Georgina tried to suppress her trembling impatience as the woman opened several drawers in search of a key, then shuffled sideways from behind the desk.

'I knew something wasn't right with him,' she continued as she led Georgina down the corridor. 'He seemed off when he arrived . . . Paranoid . . .'

They reached a door marked with a copper 6. The woman rapped gently on the wood with her knuckles before turning the key in the lock. From inside came a puzzled 'Hello?'

Her father's voice. Georgina tensed.

The mousy-haired woman mouthed, 'Good luck,' then walked away, leaving the door ajar.

From behind it, Jimmy called again. 'Hello? Is someone there?'

Entire body tense and coiled as a spring, Georgina pushed the door open and walked into the room.

40

It was a small room with a single bed. Jimmy was lying fully dressed on the duvet. When Georgina walked in, his expression of shock was so exaggerated it might have been comical under other circumstances. 'Georgina. How did you ...'

'He's not here, is he?' Georgina's hope died as she looked around the sparsely furnished room. 'Where's Cody?'

'Cody?' Jimmy sat up against the pillows. He looked exhausted, grey as old cloth, as if every drop of his usual cheeriness had been wrung from him. 'Why would Cody be here?'

'Because he's missing! Cody's missing! You're telling me you didn't know?'

'He ... *What?* Missing? What d'you mean?'

His shock and disbelief were clearly unfeigned. But it wasn't enough to convince Georgina that her father's behaviour and Cody's kidnapping were unrelated.

The photograph of Jimmy and the black-haired girl that

she'd taken with her to question Billy was still in her coat pocket. She took it out and laid it on the bed.

'Who is she, Dad?'

Jimmy looked at the photo. Real fear crossed his face.

'Why are you asking me this?' he said. 'What's going on?'

'Don't question me! *ANSWER ME!*' Georgina heard herself shouting, screaming as she had never screamed in her life. The words were torn from her, scraping her throat on their way out. 'Tell me who she is! *She's taken him!* She's taken Cody!'

'No.' Jimmy stared, horrified, at the sepia-toned image of his teenage self and the smiling girl. '*No.* She couldn't have ... she wouldn't ...'

'She has! She's the one who called you before your heart attack, right?' Georgina could see all the pieces of the puzzle she'd missed before. Jimmy's long-ago girlfriend wasn't dead. She was back. 'You told me it was Billy, and I didn't question it – even when I saw Billy and it was clear he was too sick to have been gossiping on the phone – because I trusted you. But it was her, wasn't it?'

She could see it. A voice from the past. A shock that sent her father sinking to the floor, clutching his chest.

'You're right ... she called me,' Jimmy mumbled, disorientated. 'But there's no way she's taken Cody ... You've gotten this mixed up.'

'Those toffees you love, with the golden wrappers. She used to eat the same ones when you were young, didn't she?' He nodded dumbly. 'She's been buying them for Cody! She's been telling him she wants to be his grandmother!'

Jimmy's face turned from grey to white.

'Oh Jesus, no,' he said. 'Jesus, Mary and Joseph, no.'

Georgina got down on her knees beside the bed. She grabbed his hands.

'I know she was your girlfriend. I know you got her pregnant and she was sent to a home. So just tell me—'

'My *girlfriend*?' Jimmy shook his head. 'Georgina, no. You've got it all wrong. I didn't get anyone ... Christ, how could you think ...'

He broke off. Georgina waited. When Jimmy spoke again, his voice was hoarse.

'Her name is Anne McGrath,' he said.

'Anne *McGrath*? What, were you married to her?'

'No.' Jimmy took one more look at the photo, at the girl's carefree freckled face and his own youthful, unlined features. Then he turned his ageing, watery eyes up to his daughter.

'She's my sister.'

41

'Your sister?' Georgina was momentarily blindsided. 'You don't have a sister.'

'I did. I do.' Jimmy heaved himself up on the pillows a little. 'Billy was the youngest. Anne was in the middle. A year younger than me.'

'But why—' Georgina stopped herself. No time. She raised her phone to her ear. Jimmy listened, hollow-eyed, to her conversation with the police. 'Anne McGrath ... My father's estranged sister ... Yes ... Yes ... No ... 44 Clonliffe Road.'

She thrust the phone at Jimmy, who answered some further questions. No, he had no idea how to find Anne. He hadn't seen her in fifty years. Yes, he and Georgina would wait for the police here.

He put the phone down. 'They're on their way, Georgina ... Georgina?'

She knelt on the carpet, unmoving, in a state of shock.

The hope that Cody would be here had been the only thing carrying her. Now a kind of paralysis gripped her along with the realisation that she had no idea where to go next. No idea how to find her son.

'I never wanted you to know,' Jimmy whispered. 'What happened back then. I locked all that away in a box at the back of my mind. Thought I'd take it to the grave with me. Even your mother didn't know.'

Georgina didn't respond. She couldn't. But Jimmy kept talking. It was as if the box he spoke of was in the room with them, finally creaking open, dust and decades-old secrets spilling out.

'Anne and I were born within a year of each other. Did everything together. She was brilliant fun. She'd climb any tree, steal a pound from our father's wallet so we could buy sweets ... She was a bit like Cody that way. I can't conceive of the woman that girl's grown up to be. In my mind she's still fifteen.

'I was the first person she told. Our parents ... they were wealthy, proud ... concerned with their position in society. Anne was under no illusion they'd support her. The night she crept into my room to tell me, when I said, "You're *pregnant*?", she hushed me even though I was whispering. She was terrified.'

Georgina turned her head towards him. Her father was staring past her, his eyes fixed on the wall.

'When I asked who the father was, she wouldn't say. For the next few weeks, I was half embarrassed to look at Anne. A baby, growing in her belly! Whose baby was it? What would happen now?'

Georgina was listening intently now. Perhaps there would

be some detail in this story that would help the police find Anne. Find Cody.

'Then one morning, my mother walked in on her changing. Saw the bump. God, the fighting and screaming ... I saw my father drag Anne across the kitchen by the hair, and, when I tried to stop him, got a black eye for my troubles. I was a big lad at sixteen, but it was my father I got my size from, and at forty he'd lost none of his strength.'

For the first time since he started his story, Jimmy looked at Georgina.

'My earliest memory is of my father hitting me,' he said quietly. 'In public, in a shop. I was four. He clouted me over the head so viciously that I wet myself in terror. I've long since forgotten what I did wrong, but I've never forgotten the puddle on the shop floor. I've never forgotten the shock and humiliation.'

Georgina couldn't breathe. Jimmy went on:

'She wouldn't tell them who the father was, at first. She was stubborn. I sat in my room, listening to the shouting go on for hours. But eventually I heard her coming up the stairs, and I knew she'd told. Our father's fists had a way of knocking the fight out of a person.

'Nobody filled me in. But the next afternoon, our aunt paid us a visit.

'I've never told you about my aunt and uncle, have I? I try not to mention them. They didn't have any kids of their own, and we would go to stay with them from time to time. I don't remember liking my aunt much. She was a cold woman. All I remember about my uncle, really – from before this – is that we used to play hurling together.'

Georgina was stock-still.

'My aunt wouldn't call Anne by name. *That tramp*, she kept calling her. We were all summoned to the front room – except Billy, who was only twelve. He was told to go out and play. He went willingly, frightened by the atmosphere in the house.

'Anne stood in the middle of the room like she was on trial. Our uncle wasn't present, but his wife was ready to defend him. She said that Anne was a whore, that some time with the nuns would be good for her even if she wasn't pregnant. She said our uncle had been drunk, that Anne had tempted him . . . all the things I recognise now as the stories predators tell when they're caught. But at sixteen, Georgina, I didn't understand. I just thought – our *uncle*?

'Anne tiptoed into my room that night and tried to tell me more. "I didn't let him, Jimmy," she said. "The last time we went to stay with them, he made me."

'God forgive me, Georgina, but I didn't want to know. I wanted to pretend none of this was happening. I wanted it to be a month before, when I didn't know anything was growing in Anne's belly and I was playing hurling with my uncle and everything was normal.

'Anne said, "Ma and Dad don't believe me. They're sending me away, and they said they won't let me come back again."

'I didn't think our parents meant that last bit. I knew they'd send Anne to a home, some grim place where pregnant girls were hidden away by the nuns. And I knew she'd come back without a baby – keeping the baby just wasn't done, not in nice families like ours. But I thought she would come back.'

Jimmy spoke fast.

'The parish priest came to collect her the next morning. "It's the best place, Anne," he told her. "For a girl like you."

She sobbed and argued. When our parents were unmoved, she turned to me. "Jimmy, please," she said. "Jimmy, don't let them."

'It was too much to bear. I turned to my father, but before I could speak, he had my arm in this vice-like grip. He said: "Shut your mouth, Jimmy, or I'll break your arm. Now go up to your room and close the door. And don't breathe a word of this to anyone, ever, or I'll kill you."

'I did as I was told. I turned my back on my sister and walked up the stairs. When my father's temper got like that ... somewhere inside, I was four years old, pissing on a shop floor again.

'I was lying on my bed when Anne was loaded into the car. I heard her crying. I heard the car drive away.

'I never saw my sister again.

'When Billy arrived home, he demanded to know, with all his twelve-year-old defiance, where Anne was. Our father hit him so hard he loosened two teeth. That was the last time Anne's name was mentioned in our house.' Jimmy paused, then said in a voice so low it was barely audible, 'Our uncle was invited around for Christmas dinner that year.'

There was a silence. Georgina could hear cars on the street. A child's shout. When it became clear Jimmy was finished, she asked, 'Why would she want to take Cody?'

'Because all her life she's been alone.' Jimmy closed his eyes. 'She ran away from the nuns and tried to come home. I heard my parents discussing it. She came to the house while Billy and I were at school. They turned her away at the door.

'They said she went to England. A lot of young people went to England in those days, to find a bit of work, to try to survive ...'

Georgina had thought she had no room left for shock, but she'd been wrong. A fresh stab hit her as several pieces of information fell into place.

'And you haven't seen her in fifty years? Are you telling me you never tried to find her?'

Jimmy kept his eyes shut.

'Every day of my life,' he whispered, 'I've thought of her.'

'But you never went looking for her? Never even *tried*?'

'I was ashamed.' Jimmy had never cried in front of his daughter. Not even at Rose's funeral. But tears leaked from under his closed eyelids now. 'And with every year I didn't look for her, the shame grew worse. What would I have said to her, after all that time? How could I ever have apologised enough?'

He began to sob.

'When I heard her voice on the phone, I thought I was going to collapse then and there. As it turned out, I managed to hang in till the end of the conversation. She told me her baby was a boy. "I only had one child," she said. "Like you. But they took mine away from me."'

'She said, "I should have been a mother, I should have been a grandmother. But look at me now. I'm all alone. My son's out there somewhere. I'll never know him. While *you* . . . You get everything, but you don't deserve it."' Jimmy repeated the words as though he might believe them himself. '"*You're* the one who deserves to be alone!"'

'In the hospital, when I woke to find that photo by my bed . . . It was like the past was chasing me. I ran. I wasn't thinking straight . . . '

I should have been a grandmother. Georgina thought of Mark's words: *Cody was so happy to see her!* And that card: *Lots of love, Granny xxx.*

'How can this be real, Georgina? How can Anne have taken Cody? She wouldn't hurt him, I'm sure of it ...' The shock seemed to have sent Jimmy's mind wandering. 'Our grandparents were always kind to us. They were the ones who gave us those toffees in the golden wrappers. We spent summers on their farm in Kerry. I remember playing hide-and-seek with Anne and Billy among the haystacks ...'

Georgina checked the time. The police would be here soon, but what good was that? She had nothing to tell them. Despite everything she'd learnt, she still had no idea where Anne had taken Cody.

'Dad, can you think of any place she might have brought him?'

In that same far-off voice Jimmy said, 'I feel sure that I'll wake up any minute and this'll all have been a bad dream.'

'Dad, please try to think. You said your grandparents were kind. When they came up to visit you in Dublin, did they ever take you for days out?'

'Yes, sometimes. They'd take us to Howth Head on the train. Me and Anne loved those days. On the way home, we got chips.'

'Was there anywhere else that—'

She stopped. She went still. *Howth*.

Something was coming back to her. The conversation she'd had with Anthony, earlier that afternoon. A lifetime ago.

She recalled Anthony's voice: *I'm taking Lily to Howth ... there's a market on there ... good for kiddies.*

And Patrick's: *His new granny promised she'd buy him candyfloss.*

Howth Head. A peninsula off north Dublin. A pretty seaside village. A place where Anne had happy memories with her grandparents.

And a market, where candyfloss might be sold.

Georgina leapt to her feet. 'I think I know where she's taken him.'

Jimmy looked dazed. 'Where are you . . .'

'When the Guards get here, tell them everything you just told me.'

'Georgina, wait,' Jimmy said brokenly. 'I'm sorry. I can't bear . . . Forgive me, Georgina. Please forgive me.'

But Georgina was already rushing from the room, leaving her father among the dust of his scattered memories.

42

Georgina left Jimmy's room in a state of shock that rendered the whole world unfamiliar. Everything seemed warped at the edges, unreal. It felt like she was hallucinating, like nothing would ever be the same again.

She broke into a run. Past the mousy-haired woman at the desk, who looked up, confused, out of the B&B and down the street. She leapt into her car.

Memories kept coming to her. Jimmy, refusing to watch *The Magdalene Sisters*. Jimmy, holding out a jar of gold-wrapped toffees. Jimmy, constantly discouraging her from visiting Billy in the nursing home. Georgina understood now. Her father had been afraid that Billy, in his confused state, would let something slip that would bring the half-a-century-old secret into the present.

As she pulled out from the kerb, she called Bren and let him know she was going to Howth.

'You're *what*? Georgina, what the fuck are you doing? The Guards are going to be at the B&B any second now. *Turn back!*'

'Have they found Anne McGrath?'

But her hopes that the police would have put the name through some database and pulled up an address were smashed.

'No, but they're going to the B&B and they're expecting you to be there!'

Georgina kept her foot on the accelerator.

'How will that help? I don't know anything my dad doesn't! But if she brought Cody to Howth . . . '

The phone was commandeered by the now irate-sounding Guard she had spoken to earlier. He ordered her to go back to the B&B. His colleagues, he informed her, had just arrived there. 'You're not helping us by doing this.'

I learnt the kidnapper's identity, Georgina thought. That's information we wouldn't have if I'd stayed put.

'It's where her grandparents used to take her. And it ties into Patrick's comment about candyfloss . . . ' She ran through her theory. Again the Guard urged her to turn around. Georgina made some conciliatory sounds for the sake of ending the call, but after hanging up she continued speeding towards the coast, driving like a lunatic. If a cop car tried to pull her over now, she'd only step down harder on the accelerator.

Turn back? When she knew the most likely place this unstable woman had taken her son?

There was no force in the world strong enough to compel Georgina to turn around now.

Howth Head was a peninsula, jutting out from the coast of Dublin into the Irish Sea. With a pretty village on the hill, a harbour, and a spectacular view from the summit, it was a popular spot among Dublin families for days out. People brought their kids for strolls along the pier or hikes up the hill.

They'd take us to Howth Head on the train. Me and Anne loved those days.

Large portions of the headland, too mountainous and craggy to be built on, remained untamed. Sheer sea cliffs and hills of wild gorse were edged by rocky, rugged beaches. At the end of the peninsula stood an isolated lighthouse, casting its lonely beam across the water.

It was in this direction that Georgina drove, along the coast road, away from the bustle and noise of Dublin's city centre. The night sky was clearing. The moon was huge. The sea stretched out inky black to her right.

I'm coming, Cody. Fast as I can.

It was hard for her to focus on anything other than the overwhelming terror she felt for her child. Her blood was pounding in her ears, and every beat of her thudding heart screamed Cody's name. But somewhere in the background, other thoughts jumbled about, thoughts that Georgina couldn't begin to process. Information she knew would take months, maybe years, to wrap her head around.

A teenage girl arriving in a strange country. Homeless, penniless, alone. Hoping, perhaps, that her big brother would come looking for her. While he never did. Just settled down, got a comfortable job, got married, had a child of his own – and never breathed her name again. Buried her memory as if she was a shameful secret.

Now those lies were splitting open, cracks spreading, their foundation shattering, and this woman had taken Cody, *she'd taken Cody . . .*

Forgive me, Jimmy had said. But Georgina couldn't even begin to think about that.

Let her get her child back safely. Then they could talk about forgiveness.

43

The traffic grew thicker as she reached Howth Harbour. 'Come *on*! Move!' Georgina thumped a fist against the steering wheel as she was forced to slow to a crawl.

By the picturesque waterfront, the market was in full flow. Chip vans, food stalls, a packed car park. People crowded the concrete: couples hand-in-hand, parents shouting at small children to stay close. The sky had cleared. The moon hung huge and white over the pier and the boats moored at the water's edge.

The car in front of her moved slowly, searching for a parking spot. Swearing, Georgina pulled onto the kerb and parked haphazardly on double yellow lines.

She leapt out, slammed the door, and stared out at the melee. How was she ever going to find them in this?

And if she *did* find them, would she be able to deal with Anne by herself?

But her next thought was simply *Cody*, just her son's name

on a single beat, and with it came the calm knowledge that she would do anything necessary to get him safely away.

She started off towards the food stalls. Shouts and laughter carried on the cold air. Her eyes scanned the crowd desperately. There were children in all directions – laughing, running, playing; or tired, being carried, heads resting on parents' shoulders.

But she didn't see the face she was looking for.

A child screamed. Georgina spun around, but it was a little girl, mouth stretched open into a wail. Her chocolate-covered treat had hit the ground. 'I want *another*!' she sobbed. Georgina spun in a different direction: a bunch of teenagers passed, laughing, all teeth in the dark. Faces seemed to rush by faster and faster.

But still no sign of her son.

She walked back towards the car park. It was darker here, away from the light of the food vans and restaurant fronts. She stared furiously at the passing crowds, her eyes picking out the shapes of children, searching and searching.

Maybe they weren't here at all. Panic was rising, the fear that she was like a dog chasing its own tail, spinning fruitlessly . . . But she bit that fear down and tried to remain calm. She needed a course of action. Should she try walking to the pier, or should she double back and . . .

That was when she saw him.

Cody was standing at the far end of the car park. He was in animated conversation with a grey-haired woman who had her back to Georgina. The woman was opening the door of a blue car.

Cody.

His tousled dark hair, his bright eyes, his happy chocolate-smudged face. Alive, well and right there.

Every atom of Georgina's being wanted to shout, scream, run to her son. It took everything she had to restrain that instinct. If she caught the woman's – Anne's – attention, she might throw Cody into the car and speed away up the hill before Georgina could reach them.

She forced herself to approach slowly, keeping to the grassy verge and the shadows. If she walked up the brightly lit centre of the car park, Anne would recognise her. She'd been watching their house. She knew Georgina's face.

Anne half turned in Georgina's direction as Cody climbed into the back of the car. Georgina was acutely aware of each step she took. Was this a natural gait? Did she look suspicious?

Cody was in the backseat now.

There were no more than ten cars between them and, seen more clearly, Anne did not look as elderly as Georgina had imagined. She was Jimmy's younger sister, of course, and that didn't make her enormously old – though Cody would have referred to any older grey-haired female as an 'old woman', his seven-year-old eyes unable to differentiate between people in their sixties or those in their eighties.

Anne wore jeans and a red fleece. Her grey hair was short, but unkempt and straggly. She looked stocky.

She glanced up suddenly, her gaze sweeping all around. Georgina's heart froze, but she forced herself to keep walking at the same pace, head slightly down. *Act natural. Stay calm.*

Anne's attention returned to the car. It was a battered-looking blue Volvo. Cody was frowning in innocent concentration, eating something chocolate-covered off a stick. Anne's mouth was moving, saying something to him as she leant in to buckle his seat belt. Georgina couldn't make out the words, but she was close enough to see Anne ruffle Cody's hair affectionately.

Four cars' distance now.

Anne looked around again, and this time, Georgina was too close to hope she wouldn't be recognised. She dropped into a crouch, pretending to tie her shoelace.

Her heart was in her mouth. Had it worked? Would she do better to jump up and rush them?

Then she heard the voices. Drifting towards her, distant but audible. Cody's clear, beloved voice:

'. . . the best holiday ever? And chocolate for breakfast every day?'

'The best holiday *ever*.'

Anne spoke with a faint British tinge after all her years in England. Her conversational voice was a jarring shock to Georgina's senses.

'You'll love Kerry,' that voice continued. 'You can have chocolate for breakfast, lunch and dinner if you like. You can do whatever you want. Maybe we'll go to England afterwards, would you like that?'

For the first time in her life, Georgina understood the phrase *her blood ran cold*. There was a roaring in her ears. Cody was saying something in response, but she couldn't decipher the words.

She straightened up. Anne was getting into the Volvo. In a moment she would be driving, taking Cody away.

Georgina broke into a run.

Anne looked up, her blue eyes – the same deep blue as Jimmy's, as Cody's – wide with surprise. If she had collected herself immediately, she would have had just enough time to sit down and slam the door before Georgina could stop her.

But she didn't.

Too late, Anne tried to jump into the driver's seat, but Georgina collided with her, grabbing her wrists.

With surprising strength, Anne slammed Georgina back against the car. Then the two women were grappling, desperately. Somewhere in the background, Georgina heard Cody's startled voice: 'Mam?'

'Cody!' she cried, and then her feet slipped as Anne threw her weight against her. Georgina fell backwards, hard, against the hood of the car. The sky stretched above her, the moon huge – then Anne's face loomed into view.

'You're *ruining* it!' Her eyes were glassy.

Georgina struggled, but Anne was heavy on top of her. Cody was calling, frightened.

'Mammy!'

Anne twisted sideways, using her weight and a strategically placed foot to send Georgina sliding to the ground. Before she could get her balance, Anne's fist struck her hard on the side of the head. While she was half Anne's age, Georgina had never been in a physical fight in her life.

She hit the concrete.

Cody was shouting. Georgina pulled herself to her feet. Turning to face the car, she registered the clutter on the seats (a sleeping bag, a bare pillow, crumbs, fast-food wrappers, clothes) and realised this battered car was Anne's home.

Anne was in the driver's seat, about to slam the door. *No.* Georgina twisted around and reached out a hand to stop her . . .

Anne's eyes followed the path of Georgina's hand. She timed it perfectly, waiting until just the right moment. Then she slammed the door, hard, onto Georgina's fingers.

For half a heartbeat, Georgina felt nothing.

Then she screamed.

The door opened again, allowing her broken hand to slip out. Cody was shrieking hysterically.

'You're ruining it!' Anne shouted at her again. 'You're ruining everything!'

Georgina could only gasp and clutch at her already ballooning fingers. Anne slammed the door shut. Through the glass, Georgina heard Cody's wail.

'I don't want to go to Kerry any more! I want my mam! Let me out! *Let me out!*'

Anne reversed. The car shot backwards, over the grass, scattering crowds, causing screams, and smashed into a restaurant front. A man who had been smoking outside vaulted out of the way just in time.

Georgina found her voice. She screamed, '*Cody!*'

The car turned and sped off up the hill, the broken back bumper dragging on the concrete.

Cody.

A crowd was gathering. Georgina swayed, clutching her hand. She could only babble incoherently: 'My son . . . my son . . .'

'Should I call the Guards?' a stranger offered.

Georgina sagged against a nearby car, overwhelmed. People were asking her questions, but she could barely hear them. Oh God, she'd failed. She'd let that woman take her child.

With an effort, she pulled herself up and set off in the direction of her car. 'Are you okay?' someone tried to ask, but Georgina stumbled past, trying not to think about how she would drive with an injured hand. Cody's screaming rang in her ears. She could feel her fingers pulsing and hot, the skin stretching as they swelled.

She was almost at her car when she heard the commotion. Car horns blaring. People shouting. Someone nearby yelled, like it was one word, 'Oh-my-God-*look-out*!'

Georgina turned around, and, like a slow-motion scene from a movie, she saw it.

The blue Volvo was speeding back down the hill.

Pedestrians flung themselves out of the way as the car swerved up onto the path. Bursting through the low barricade, it drove straight onto the pier. People scattered before it. The night air was thick with screams. But Georgina couldn't scream. Couldn't move. Motionless as a mannequin in a shop window, she could only stare as the blue Volvo shot down the pier, off the edge –

– and splashed into the black water below.

44

All around, chaos erupted.

Shouts. Screams. Calls for someone to dial 999.

Georgina began to run.

The world flew past in a ragged blur. Among the strangers' faces, she glimpsed a familiar one: Anthony. He had an arm around his frightened-looking granddaughter. 'Georgina?'

She raced by. Across the car park. Onto the pier. She pulled off her coat as she ran, letting it fall behind her. She yanked her top over her head too and cried out – it jarred her crushed fingers, and the pain was a flash of fire.

A small crowd had gathered at the end of the pier. One woman was taking a video of the sinking car on her phone. A young man was undressing ostentatiously but seemed in no great rush to jump in.

In her jeans and bra, oblivious to the freezing air, Georgina elbowed her way through the crowd. Kicking off her shoes, she shoved past the half-dressed young man and the woman taking the video, causing her phone to tumble from her hand – '*Hey!*' But Georgina heard nothing over the screaming in her mind, howling her son's name in time to the desperate beat of her heart:

Cody-Cody-Cody-Cody –

Several feet below, the car's blue–and–silver metal was still visible for one horribly taunting moment. Then the inky black water swallowed it greedily.

Cody-Cody-Cody –

'Oh my God,' said a female voice. The young man who had undressed was beginning a slow descent of the rocks at the pier end. Another voice, a man's, said impotently, 'Somebody *do* something.'

Georgina clambered down the rocks in seconds and hurled herself into the icy water.

The cold hit her like a sledgehammer. Crushing her chest, cutting her skin. She rose above the surface and gasped, dragging air into her shocked lungs. She took several deep breaths, then dived down again.

Underwater, she was groping blind. She tried opening her eyes against the burning salt, but it was futile – she could see nothing but black. Her uninjured hand found the surface of the car and slid across it, seeing by touch. Smooth metal, hard edges.

The back of the car. It was sinking nose-first.

She kicked up for air again. As she broke the surface, some-one else emerged from the water beside her: the young man had jumped in.

'I can't get the door open!' he yelled up to the crowd, pan-icked. 'I can't!'

Several people were filming this on their phones now. Others were shouting advice:

'The doors won't open till the car's filled with water!'

'It's something to do with pressure!'

'Break the window!'

'No, that won't help . . .'

Georgina took a deep breath and dived back below. Her blood beat the rhythm in her ears, the old familiar rhythm that was perhaps all it had beaten since the day he was born, risen only to this desperate screaming crescendo now his life was in danger.

Cody-Cody-Cody-Cody-Cody –

Her good hand slid along the metal in the dark until she found a handle. She pulled, hard, but the door didn't budge.

The doors won't open till the car's filled with water.

Was that true? Georgina thought it might be. It was stored somewhere in the back of her mind, along with similar bits of trivia, like how to survive on a desert island – the kind of information you picked up but never dreamt you'd use. Because the application belonged in nightmares.

She swam up for air and dived down again. Submerged in the salty water, limbs flailing in the dark, she found the metal, the door, the handle.

She pulled, and this time it opened.

A stream of bubbles escaped her mouth. Her feet begged to kick back up, to oxygen, but instead she reached inside the car. Her fingers touched a seat belt, sodden material . . . Was that clothes she could feel? But she needed *air* –

This time she came up screaming.

'Cody!' She floundered in the water. It was growing harder to swim. The cold was unbelievable, her limbs numb, her injured hand agonising. '*Cody!*'

'Careful!' The young man was above the surface too. 'You'll sink . . .'

And in her panic, she did. Her head went under, salt water filling her mouth. She resurfaced spluttering.

The young man swam a few strokes towards her. 'Are you okay?'

'Forget me! There's a child in the car – a boy . . .'

A murmur rippled through the watching crowd. *Oh-my-God-did-she-just-say-a-child?*

The young man's eyes widened. Georgina would never forget his shocked face, his red hair and plentiful freckles, how pale his skin glistened in the moonlight.

In the periphery of her vision, she saw a familiar figure push to the front of the crowd. '*Georgina!*' Anthony shouted.

But Georgina couldn't waste a second. She filled her lungs with air and dived under.

She had to swim further to reach the car this time. She pushed *down*, *down*, already feeling the lack of oxygen. She and Bren had timed themselves holding their breath once. Bren had made it to forty-four seconds, Georgina only to thirty-eight. She would have to do better than that now, have faith that her body, pushed to necessity by extreme circumstances, would deliver.

She found the back of the car. The door had closed. As Georgina pulled it open, she could *feel* the car sinking.

She slid inside.

Blindly, she groped around. The tight space was thick with sodden material, rubbish . . . Her chest was tightening, the need for air gathering, but she reached desperately into the dark.

Her hand collided with warm flesh.

She knew instantly that she was touching Anne. The floating limb was too thick to be Cody's, the doughy skin too soft under her fingertips. She was gripping Anne's wrist – and it was twitching.

The realisation that she was trapped in a sinking car with a dying woman struck Georgina.

She opened her mouth to scream and a stream of bubbles escaped.

Air. She needed air.

She released Anne's arm and went flailing back. Her leg caught in something soft – the sleeping bag? Her good hand, groping behind her, found the door closed. The pressure of the water as the car descended had pushed it shut.

The last of the air bubbled from her lungs as she tried to twist around and open the door. The pressure on her chest was incredible. *Don't breathe in*, she tried to tell her lungs, *it's not air, just water, NOT-AIR-JUST-WATER*, but her body was going to betray her, she was going to inhale, she could feel it. The sodden sleeping bag was tangled around her legs. She was trapped. And *Cody-Cody-Cody*, she hadn't saved Cody –

For a moment, Georgina wanted to give up.

Then the door opened. Strong arms grabbed her and pulled her from the car, then up-up-up to the surface.

For the length of that first breath, Georgina knew nothing but the sheer relief of air filling her lungs. But by the time she'd finished exhaling, the chorus in her mind was roaring again.

Cody-Cody-Cody-Cody –

She thrashed in the water. The pain and shock and terror would have caused her to sink if it wasn't for her rescuer's powerful arms.

'Georgina, stop struggling! I've got you.'

Big arms. Faded tattoos. A familiar voice.

Anthony.

Turning, Georgina saw that Anthony was wearing an expression of terrible sympathy. The young man was above the surface too, white-faced and desperate-looking. But where was Cody?

'Cody was in that car,' she gasped. 'Where is he? Did you save him?'

She saw the answer in their faces.

The world went dark.

45

Anthony must have pulled her from the water, although later, Georgina had no memory of that happening. The next thing she was aware of was sitting on concrete, surrounded by people clamouring, sirens wailing, blue lights flashing. Somebody had wrapped a silvery-plastic thermal blanket around her. 'The coastguard is here,' a stranger's voice was saying, but Georgina knew it was too late for that. It had started being too late a while ago.

All around was chaos and shouting. Below, the water was black and still and calm.

Several feet away, Anthony, also wrapped in a thermal blanket, was trying to maintain his composure for the sake of a scared Lily, who pleaded, 'Granda, I want to go home . . .' The young man with the red hair and freckled face, who had tried and failed to save her son, sat with a silver blanket around his shoulders too, and a paper cup of some hot beverage in his hands. He did not drink from it, just stared at the rising steam.

Georgina had not known thermal blankets were made of this odd metallic material. She watched the way hers shimmered in the moonlight instead of listening to the words coming at her. 'Can you hear me, Georgina? Georgina?' A policewoman kept trying to ask her questions until another Guard, an older man, snapped, 'Give her some space, would you?' An ambulance driver kept saying, 'The little boy? The little boy was in the car?' They were all here now – the police, Bren, Kelly-Anne, the coastguard – but too late.

She could hear Bren crying, a terrible sound, but Georgina felt removed from it all. She watched as if from a great distance as Bren leapt into the sea and was dragged out again, as he cast around the pier in his freezing and sodden clothes, ignoring offers of a blanket, calling for his son. She could imagine the everyday Bren observing this scene and shaking his head, commenting: 'A classic example of denial.'

Kelly-Anne stood a few feet away and answered the Guards' questions when it became clear Georgina wasn't capable of doing so. 'A great-aunt ... Estranged ...' Kelly-Anne was crying too. But Georgina was dry-eyed. She felt detached, as if she were floating somewhere far above. Even when Bren staggered over to her, like a drunk or a man who had suffered a terrible injury, and tried to hold her, she just sat there, indifferent. She was drifting away towards the full moon. Nothing was real. The chorus of *Cody-Cody-Cody* had stopped, finally, and inside her was just silence. Hollow, empty rooms. No adrenaline, no urgency, no need for it any more.

There was a gentle touch on her shoulder. A female medic with a kind face crouched beside her, asking questions. Georgina couldn't make out the words. It was like listening through a thick pane of glass.

'. . . get you home . . . in shock . . . '

Disjointed bits of sentences reached her distantly. She didn't understand, didn't care. The moon was huge above.

The medic took her arm and she allowed herself to be half carried along. A reporter stepped into Georgina's path, trying to shove a microphone in her face, but a hand decorated with long fake nails flew out and slapped the microphone aside.

'Back off and leave her alone,' Kelly-Anne snapped, advancing like she intended to take the reporter and his entire camera crew on single-handedly. The medic steered Georgina around them and in the direction of an ambulance.

Somewhere in the distance there was shouting. A murmur ran through the crowd.

Georgina didn't feel even the dullest curiosity. Curiosity was beyond her. Someone was calling her name.

'Georgina! *Georgina!*'

But she didn't care. There was nothing to care about any more.

Then she heard:

'Cody!'

Something stirred inside her, but with great reluctance, not daring to hope. People were running towards the hill. She turned her head in the same direction –

– and saw the small figure, alone, trailing down the slope. *Cody.*

Georgina's entire body sang her son's name. Her heart seemed to resume beating. Blood flowed back into her limbs, right to her fingertips. Her broken hand began to burn again. Colour rushed back into the world.

She was tottering a little as she ran towards him. Other people got there first, but they moved aside for her. Her blanket had fallen off, but she barely noticed the cold. In her bra and jeans she fell to her knees and gathered her son into her arms. Cody was crying. There was a graze on his forehead, but otherwise he seemed unharmed.

'I'm sorry, Mam,' he kept saying. 'I'm sorry.'

Georgina couldn't speak. She held onto him like she would never let him go. She forgot the pain in her hand. She forgot the panic she had felt trapped in the sinking car. She forgot about everything but Cody, Cody, Cody. He was all that mattered in the world.

Then Bren was there too, his arms wrapped around them both, sobbing. He squeezed them so tightly it was painful. He kept saying, 'Oh, thank God, thank God. What happened, Cody? What happened?' and then hugging his son so hard he didn't have a chance to answer.

Kelly-Anne appeared and wrapped her faux-fur coat around Georgina's bare shoulders. Somewhere in the background, someone was taking photos – the *click-click* just audible – and Kelly-Anne turned on them ferociously:

'D'you have no respect, no? Give them a bit of space. Yeah, that's right, you too. Put that phone away. And see *you* . . .'

'Excuse me, I'm a professional. We're from the *Sunday Star*.'

'I don't care where you're from. If you don't put that camera away, I'll break it over your head. Give this family some privacy.'

The concrete was rough against Georgina's knees, Bren's head was pressing into hers so hard it was painful, but she didn't want to move. Above, the winter moon glowed bright. And below, the Guards set about dragging a battered car from the water – a car that contained only one body.

46

Later, the Guards would tell Georgina what little they knew of Anne's life. A thumbnail sketch based on what scraps of information could be gathered.

It was not the kind of life that left much of a paper trail.

Anne McGrath never had a mortgage, a life insurance policy or a wedding certificate. She had rarely had a fixed address. Occasional periods as a registered employee were broken up by much longer periods – often years – during which, legally, Anne might not have existed at all. She'd been lost somewhere in the underbelly of society, where cash was untaxed and turned straight into food and alcohol and shelter. Where people moved from squats to hostels to sleeping bags on park benches. She had not claimed social welfare for some years, perhaps due to her chaotic life and lack of address, perhaps because the paperwork was simply too much for her. The blue Volvo she had driven had been reported stolen in Bristol eight weeks previously.

Anne's most reliable paper trail was her hospital records, and they told a bleak story. In her twenties, she had been brought to St Thomas' Hospital in London after a severe beating at the hands of her then partner. Anne was several months pregnant at the time. She lost the baby – her second lost baby, Georgina thought – and suffered internal damage so severe she was never able to have children again.

The medical records also noted Anne's stays in the public psychiatric unit, which grew longer and more frequent as she grew older. 'She was always asking for the baby she'd given up for adoption,' a nurse told the press anonymously, after the story garnered some publicity. 'Talking about finding her baby, accusing us of taking her baby ... She was obsessed.'

There were many gaps in the narrative of how the skinny girl with the freckles and mischievous smile had become the woman whose bloated body was dragged from the sea. But perhaps the most important part of the story was the beginning. The part where she ended up in a foreign country, a teenager, traumatised, destitute, alone.

And the ending, of course. They could piece that together easily enough.

They knew she had returned to Ireland and been lucid enough to look up her estranged brothers. Billy had been in a home for several years by then. But Jimmy, her big brother, her long-ago best friend, who'd walked away from her back then and never tried to make amends – he had a good life. A big house. A loving family.

It did not take much imagination to picture Anne staring hungrily across the road at the life that should have been hers.

A warm bed instead of a car to sleep in. Companionship and cosy family Christmases instead of loneliness, hospital rooms, nobody to list as an emergency contact. A grandson like Cody instead of a ragged wound in her heart.

Georgina could picture it. Anne lurking around their house, staring in the windows, making sure she left no signs of her presence. Until the day she smashed Georgina's flower-pots in a flash of petty rage so strong she forgot herself.

As time passed, Cody filled his parents in on all the parts they'd missed. They heard the story in bits and pieces until they could picture the chain of events clearly.

Cody hadn't known to be wary of Anne's erratic behav-iour. He'd been happy to meet the woman who surprised him in the park with a lollipop and promised to be his new grandmother. She was loving and kind. Anne would call the house phone and they would play the yes-or-no game. She asked questions and Cody had to answer without using the words 'yes' and 'no'.

'Are you a boy?'

'I am.'

'Are you a cat?'

'I am not!'

'What's your name?'

'Cody.'

'How do you spell that?'

'C-O-D-Y.'

'And is that your real name?'

'Yes – I mean: *it is*! It is!'

It was a surprisingly hard game, but Cody liked it. If he managed to answer without saying yes or no for a full minute, his new granny would leave sweets hidden for him in the garden. It sometimes took him many attempts to complete a full minute, but Anne always let him keep trying until he did.

When Anne explained that his parents didn't like her and that he had to pretend she existed only in his imagination – well, Cody was a mischievous child, just as Anne herself had once been. He was used to keeping secrets from adults. When he explained that his mam was getting suspicious, Anne coached him through the process of fibbing to the police if they showed up. She made it seem almost fun.

And when his new granny said she'd take him for a special day out, Cody was happy to play along. All he had to do was tell a little lie to Patrick's parents. It broke Georgina's heart to think of Cody climbing into the back of the Volvo – so innocent, so excited to be getting away with it. Not knowing that by the end of the night, that car would be sinking to the sea floor.

The day was fun, Cody said. Until Georgina appeared and Anne hurt her. Then it all went bad. When Anne reversed the car and went speeding up the hill, she had been shouting things and driving too fast. It was scary. Cody was frightened. He told New Granny he didn't want to go to Kerry any more. He wanted to go back. He wanted his mam.

Anne had stopped the car so hard that Cody, who had taken off his seat belt, flew forward and bumped his forehead. She turned around, told him to stop his screaming, and slapped him across the face. Cody, who had never been struck by an adult, was momentarily stunned into silence. Then, at the same moment, he and Anne both burst into tears.

'I'm sorry, Cody,' she told him, over and over. 'I'm sorry.' She tried to hug him, but he pulled away. She cried harder. 'I'm a bad grandmother. I've ruined everything.'

She reached for him again, and he kicked at her.

'I don't want you! I want Mam!'

Anne looked sad at first, but when he lashed out a second time, she got angry.

'You don't want me? Fine. *Fine!*' And she leant into the back, reached over him and opened the car door. 'Get out then,' she said, crying. 'Go.'

Cody had clambered out onto the side of a road he didn't know. He was even more scared then, being in this strange place. 'Don't leave me here,' he begged.

But Anne had driven away and left him alone.

As Cody told his parents later, all he could think to do was to walk back in the direction they had come. It was very dark, and he kept imagining he saw shapes moving in the gardens he passed. He walked as fast as he could.

Eventually the road led him to a village and the top of the hill. At the bottom of the hill, there were a lot of police cars and people shouting. Scared and disorientated, he had walked doggedly in the direction of those blue lights, sure that one of the grown-ups would help him find his mam. 'And then all these people started running at me, and saying my name ... and then I saw you, Mam! And Dad too. And then we got to go in the Garda car.'

It was in the police car home from Howth that Cody, squeezed between his shell-shocked parents, had turned to Georgina and said: 'Mam? Where's New Granny?'

Epilogue

What little of the sky Georgina could see through the curtains was bright blue. The house smelled of toast and coffee. She could hear Bren and Cody talking downstairs.

She sat up in bed and stretched. She must have fallen asleep again. She'd woken at 7 a.m. and rolled into Bren's arms as the dawn light filtered through the curtains. They'd had morning sex, quiet but intense, Bren's hand clamped over her mouth to muffle the sounds she made at the end.

Georgina got up, walked to the window, and pulled the curtains back. The first flowers of spring were blooming. The Brazilian couple across the street were pushing their newborn baby in a pram.

Despite everything, life went on.

But some things took time to heal. Georgina's bandaged right hand gave a twinge at the thought.

Jimmy was not coping well. He seemed to have forgotten how to laugh. He didn't leave the house much these days, except to potter around the garden. He always remembered to leave food and water out for the birds now. But the sadness that hung around him was so heavy it was palpable.

'I forgive you, Dad,' Georgina had told him, many times. 'Now you need to forgive yourself.'

Last time they spoke, Jimmy told her, hesitantly, that he wanted to pay for a gravestone for Anne. He'd been anxious about Georgina's reaction. This was the woman who had abducted her child, after all.

But Georgina didn't hate Anne. Yes, she had subjected Georgina to the most terrifying hours of her life, but Anne had only been a child herself when she was raped, disowned, abandoned. During her therapy sessions, Georgina was trying to work through her confused feelings towards the woman who, in another life, would have been her loving aunt.

Her feelings towards her father were complicated too. Sometimes she still felt anger towards Jimmy, for everything he had concealed and what it had cost them, for all the things he'd failed to do.

But mostly she just felt sad for him. A painful sadness that sat behind her ribcage.

'Buy her a gravestone, Dad,' Georgina said. She didn't say *Why do for her in death what you couldn't do in life?* All she added was: 'Make sure it says *mother* on it.' Anne *had* been a mother, however brief the time she was allowed with her child. Her gravestone should reflect that.

Down on the street, Vera was bustling off somewhere, in her purple scarf and coat. Georgina waved.

Recently, Georgina had asked Vera about that strange comment she'd made about her family. *I don't really miss them at all . . .* How could she not miss her daughter, son-in-law and grandson after they'd gone from living under her roof to Australia?

'Oh don't get me wrong!' Vera hastened to say. 'I'd have rather they moved down the road than to the other side of the world. But at the same time – and don't ever tell Lorraine I said this – I'm just *so glad* to have my house to myself again.'

Georgina was stunned. Vera went on, 'I don't miss being woken by a toddler at five a.m. Or minding Sean Monday to Friday. Do I sound terrible? I love my grandson, but I already raised my own child. I never planned to spend the rest of my life raising someone else's.'

Georgina assured Vera she didn't sound terrible. She felt a little abashed at the assumptions she'd made. It had never occurred to her that Vera might have interests beyond providing free full-time childcare.

'Now I sleep in whenever I want,' said Vera. 'I watch what *I* want on TV. And I'm taking evening classes. I didn't get to finish school when I was young, you know, and always felt I'd missed out on the opportunity. Now I'm studying history, and it's just fascinating. I'm learning so much. In fact,' she'd glanced at her watch, 'I can't stand and chat too long, Georgina. I've lots of homework to do.'

And she'd trotted off, adjusting the purple scarf around her neck as she went. That evening, she'd dropped by to give Georgina a jar of home-made blackcurrant jam.

As she watched Vera disappear down the street now, Georgina heard Cody calling from downstairs. 'Mam?' And Bren saying, 'Shush, Mam's asleep . . .'

She pulled on her dressing gown, ruminating on Cody's progress. He seemed to be coping remarkably well. The child psychologist with whom he was having weekly meetings had commented on his courage and tenacity. Georgina could only hope he'd inherited his real grandmother's inner strength.

'Kids are resilient,' Bren had said recently. 'More so than adults.'

'Maybe,' Georgina replied. 'Or maybe we just don't take their distress as seriously as we take our own.' She had been determined not to do that with Cody. In the aftermath of everything, she made sure to get professional help for Cody as well as herself.

Cody drew pictures of his new granny in heaven. He had, with his incredible seven-year-old's capacity for forgiveness, got over her shouting at him, hitting him and leaving him on the side of the road. 'She did nice things mostly, Mam.' He also felt deep guilt that he hadn't allowed Anne to hug him goodbye. 'I should have given New Granny a hug. It wasn't nice to kick at her.'

'No, sweetie,' Georgina told him fiercely and repeatedly. 'Don't ever feel bad about that. You did nothing wrong. Your new granny was a very sad and mixed-up lady, and it would have taken more than a hug to make her better. Okay?'

Cody had recently drawn a picture of Anthony as a super-hero, saving his mam from the sea. Georgina felt a surge of uncomfortable emotions when she saw that drawing. She knew from Anthony's expression when Cody presented him with it that he felt similarly, but he thanked Cody gravely and promised to put the drawing on his fridge.

Lily was allowed to visit Anthony at home now. She could often be seen running around his back garden with the new rabbit – a ball of white fluff Lily had christened Snowpuff – hopping around at her feet.

Sometimes Cody and Lily would play together. It meant

everything to Georgina to see her son playing with his new friend like a normal seven-year-old.

The TV was on downstairs. Bren's muffled voice was followed by Cody's laughter. Georgina checked her phone. She had a message from Kelly-Anne:

> **Remember, spa day tomorrow!! They'll put cucumbers on your eyes and you will LIKE IT!! See you in the morning! Xx**

She laughed aloud. Tomorrow was their much-anticipated girls' day out. Kelly-Anne had booked them in for an all-day experience: facials, massages, the lot. Georgina was actually looking forward to it.

Recently, she'd been taking one full day off a week, no studying allowed. And she had been surprised to find that she was still doing just as well at college. 'Of course you are,' Bren said. 'You were burnt out before. Taking time off is good for performance. It gives your brain a chance to recharge.'

Georgina and Bren were doing better these days too. She had filled him in on everything, all the parts she hadn't told him before, including the time she'd climbed into Anthony's garden. It felt like they were on the same team again.

Bren showed her every day that he was sorry, that he'd do anything to rebuild the trust. 'As long as it takes, Georgina.' That he was committed. That he'd chosen his marriage, his family, this life.

Georgina looked around at their sunlit bedroom, the crumpled duvet. The sound of her son and husband's laughter floated up the stairs. This was the life she chose, too. Her marriage might not look exactly like she'd imagined, but it was hers.

One thing that still amazed Georgina was that Rose had never known about Anne. If such secrets could exist in a marriage as happy and enduring as her parents' . . . It helped Georgina to forgive herself for the paranoid thoughts she had had about Bren.

Jimmy had framed one of the old photos of Anne and put it on the mantelpiece. After all those years, it had finally been dusted off and brought into the light. Anne beamed out of the photograph – dark hair, freckles, crooked teeth, mischievous grin. Frozen at fifteen, in a field in Kerry in summer, beside her beloved brother, smiling into the sun.

Author's Note

The idea for this novel was sparked by a conversation I had with my mother. She was telling me stories about the Ireland of her childhood, a country radically different to the one I grew up in. Like many people of my generation, I was familiar with the history of the Magdalene laundries and the mother-and-baby homes, but it didn't feel wholly real to me. I was raised in the nineties, a time of crop tops and the Spice Girls. The repressive culture that institutionalised women for the crimes of being pregnant, being sexually active or being sexually abused seemed long-ago. 'You can't imagine what it was actually like,' my mother told me. 'You can't imagine the stigma and shame people felt.'

One of the anecdotes she shared with me was about a girl whose family wouldn't allow her to come home after she had her baby. This simple, devastating detail stuck with me. As I walked home that night, I couldn't stop thinking about how vulnerable a young person in that situation would be. Quite of its own accord, the plot of the novel took shape in my head. I saw the opening scenes: the icy park, the playground, the deserted fields. I felt the familiar shiver that runs from my spine to my fingertips when I'm struck by an idea that demands to be put on the page. When I got home, I sat down at my laptop and wrote the first two chapters on the spot.

Wrapping Anne's story up in a work of psychological suspense came naturally to me, as this is the genre in which I write. I strive to create the kinds of stories I love to read: those that balance page-turning plots with emotional depth. While Anne is an entirely fictional character, I nonetheless felt a deep sense of loyalty to her, and the chapter in which her backstory is revealed was the most difficult for me to write. I wanted to explore the issue of severed familial bonds, and how people like Jimmy ended up colluding with the oppressive, misogynistic powers that sent their loved ones off to those institutions.

As my mother says, I can't imagine what it was like back then. To the nineties-born generation, it can feel like bygone history. But eras overlap. It wasn't until 1996, the same year the Spice Girls achieved international success with their smash hit 'Wannabe', that the last Magdalene laundry was closed. Abortion remained illegal in Ireland, even in cases of rape and incest, until 2018, when the anachronistic 8th amendment to the constitution was finally repealed following a long battle by grass-roots campaigners. When my mother and other Irish people from past generations tell me stories of growing up under a hyper-conservative Catholic culture, it reminds me that those days weren't that long ago at all, and that the shadow of what was done then still stretches out across the years.

Acknowledgements

I'd like to begin by thanking Nita Pronovost at Simon & Schuster CA, without whom this book would still be a manuscript. I'd like to thank Sara Quaranta at Simon & Schuster US, whose meticulous editorial notes were invaluable, and Hannah Wann and Anna Boatman at Little, Brown, for the thoughtful notes, for championing my work so fiercely, and for all the support. I'm extremely lucky to have had the guidance of such exceptional editors.

I'd like to extend a big thank-you to all the teams behind the scenes at Simon & Schuster CA, Simon & Schuster US, and Little, Brown. A wide range of talented people are involved in the process which resulted in you holding this book in your hands, and I'm grateful to each and every one.

An enormous thank-you to my wonderful agent, Marianne Gunn O'Connor, who picked my manuscript from the slush pile and believed in me from the beginning. I'd also like to thank Alison Walsh for the early guidance and support.

To my family and friends, it's hard to know where to start. To my mother, who bought me books, to Lauren, my Theo van Gogh and biggest cheerleader, to Dylan, for always being in my corner, and to my father, who told his daughter to dream big. I love you guys beyond words. To Niamh and Darren, for exemplifying supportiveness, for everything. My achievements are yours too. To Cáit, for the unwavering belief since our schooldays. If I try to name everyone, this section will go on for pages and pages, so I'll just say this: to each of you who cheered me on at every turn, who believed in me years before I had anything published, and who celebrated my wins as if they were your own, thank you, thank you, thank you. No writer could ask to have a more supportive gang in her corner.

A Q&A with Rachel Ryan

Have you always wanted to be a writer?

Since I was a little girl. I wrote 'novels' in school copybooks from a very young age. I still have a novel that I wrote at about ten years old. It's about a girl called Alana who finds a magic pearl on a beach and ends up visiting an underwater world full of interesting sea creatures.

What was the most difficult part of writing the book, and the most rewarding?

I find the editing process to be simultaneously the most difficult and the most rewarding step. Editors force you to step outside your work and look at it from a distance, which is extremely challenging, but necessary. Perhaps the part I most enjoy is writing first drafts. That's when I can achieve what some people refer to as flow state, when the words just spill from my fingertips. That's when I'm getting to know my characters and my story.

Where did you find inspiration for your characters?

My characters tend to walk into my head quite fully formed. I can always see them vividly — it's like mentally meeting someone. Then I have to spend some time with them, getting to know them. Most of what I learn about my characters doesn't end up on the page. For example, there's a lot of Vera's backstory that didn't make it into the novel, plus a lot about Jimmy and Rose's marriage.

What are some of your writing influences?

As well as being influenced by all the psychological suspense I've ever read, *Hidden Lies* owes a lot to Gothic and horror influences, and to the places where all those genres overlap. I read backwards in that area, as I guess people tend to do when they become interested in an art form. I started out reading Erin Kelly and Stephen King, and from there found my way back to Ira Levin and Daphne du Maurier. I'm obsessed with eerie, evocative settings and a strong sense of place. I've pored over *Rosemary's Baby* and *Rebecca*. I've read my copy of *The Poison Tree* so many times it's falling apart. All of those influences have really informed my writing style. With *Hidden Lies*, I wanted to create an urban landscape with a gothic twist. I'm also very influenced by onscreen horror. I've watched *The Orphanage* and *Stranger Things* more times than I can count. Many elements of *Hidden Lies* are inspired by classic ghost-story tropes: a wronged figure from the past, a threat that only the child can see. I enjoyed playing around with those elements and building them into the plot of a psychological thriller with a human explanation for everything.

What do you enjoy doing in your spare time?

My first answer is the one that all writers give: I love to read. But it feels the most pertinent, particularly as I'm writing this on the heels of the coronavirus pandemic, when lockdown cut me off from most of the other things I love. Meeting friends in coffee shops, going hiking and getting out in nature, ambling around Dublin's city centre and idly window-shopping – all of a sudden I couldn't do any of the things I took for granted. Couldn't go swimming, couldn't go camping, couldn't meet friends for a drink and a dance. But I could still read. I could still pick up a book and be transported to another time and place. For me, that feeling of being transported is what makes reading magic. I love film, I love theatre, but I don't find any other narrative art form as utterly immersive as reading a book. That's why, despite all my varied interests and hobbies, when someone asks me what I enjoy doing, 'reading' is the first word that springs to my lips.